Roberto Clemente

Young Baseball Player

Illustrated by Meryl Henderson

Roberto Clemente

Young Baseball Player

by Montrew Dunham

ALADDIN PAPERBACKS

First Aladdin Paperbacks edition April 1997

Aladdin Paperbacks
An imprint of Simon & Schuster
Children's Publishing Division
1230 Avenue of the Americas
New York, NY 10020

Manufactured in the United States of America

14 16 18 20 19 17 15

Library of Congress Cataloging-in-Publication Data
Dunham, Montrew.
Roberto Clemente : young ball player / by Montrew Dunham.
— 1st Aladdin Paperbacks ed.
p.   cm. — (Childhood of famous Americans)
Summary: Traces the personal life and baseball career of the Puerto Rican baseball superstar, from his childhood love of the game through his professional career and untimely death to his election to the Hall of Fame in 1973.
ISBN-13: 978-0-689-81364-1   ISBN-10: 0-689-81364-3
1. Clement, Roberto, 1934–1972—Juvenile literature. 2. Baseball players—United States—Biograry—Juvenile literature. 3. Puerto Ricans—Biography—Juvenile literature. [1. Clemente, Roberto, 1934–1972. 2. Baseball players. 3. Puerto Ricans—Biography.] I. Title. II. Series: Childhood of famous Americans series.
GV865.C45D86   1997
796.357'092—dc21
[B]   96-37326
CIP   AC
0114 OFF

Dedicated to Ciudad Sportiva

I am grateful to the National Baseball Hall of Fame
and the Pittsburgh Pirates for taking the time to
answer all of my questions. —M.D.

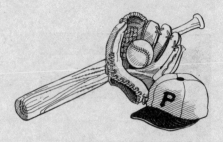

Illustrations

Numerous smaller illustrations

Contents

Roberto Clemente

Young Baseball Player

Play Ball!

ROBERTO CLEMENTE LOVED to play baseball more than anything else. Even when he didn't have a ball to play with, he and his friends hit tin cans. Often they used any kind of a stick they could find as a bat.

Roberto was born on August 18, 1934 in Puerto Rico, a sunny island in the Caribbean where people spoke Spanish. He lived in the small town of Carolina, which was near San Juan. The youngest of seven children, he had two sisters—Rosa and Ana Elise—and four brothers—Luis, Matino, Andres, and

Oswaldo. Luis and Rosa were Roberto's mother's children from her first marriage. They were much older than Roberto. Sadly, Ana Elise died when Roberto was very young.

Like most of the men in Roberto's neighborhood, the Barrio of San Anton, Roberto's father, Melchor Clemente, worked in the sugarcane fields. He worked very hard, and had been promoted to a foreman. He oversaw the work of a crew of sugarcane cutters. Even so, he did not make very much money.

In the wintertime the children went to school Mondays through Fridays, but after school and until mid-summer they helped with the work. During the day Roberto's older brothers went with their father to the fields to work, or sometimes they helped in the little store which their parents ran out of their home. Señor Clemente also had an old truck that he used to make extra money. With the truck, he hauled sugarcane or building materials or anything else that needed to be moved. Señor Clemente and his wife, Luisa, both worked very hard to have enough money to take care of their family.

One summer day, Roberto had helped his brothers Matino and Andres load the truck with sand. After they finished their work, he ran to the field across the road from his house to see if there were any boys playing baseball.

José was already there with his broomstick bat and a pile of tin cans. "Roberto, will you pitch to me?" José called.

Roberto went to the pretend pitcher's mound by the tin cans and tossed a can to José. He swung at it and missed. Their rules were that if the hitter missed, he had to be the pitcher for the other boy. But José protested, "I didn't see the can coming! Pitch another to me!"

"Okay," Roberto said, and pitched another can. This time José hit it. Roberto threw a couple more cans until José finally missed one. Now it was José's turn to pitch to Roberto.

José threw the cans high and low. Sometimes he tossed the can so crooked that Roberto had to leap to the side to swing at it. But Roberto always hit the tin can. José complained, "I always have to be the pitcher, because you never miss!"

Roberto laughed. He loved playing ball, and liked being able to hit so well. Sometimes he hit the tin cans so hard that they sailed across the field to the banana trees.

"Okay, you can be the hitter and I'll toss the cans to you," he said to José. "But first we need to pick them up." The boys scrambled all over the dusty field to pick up the many cans Roberto had hit.

They collected all the tin cans and once again placed them in a pile next to where the pitcher would stand. José grabbed the stick and ran to the batter's place. Roberto picked up a can and started to throw it to

José. In the distance he saw some of the men walking down the road. They were coming home from the sugarcane fields.

Quickly he tossed the can for José to hit, and then he turned to leave. "I need to go meet my father!" he called back over his shoulder.

Nearly every day Roberto met his father at the sugarcane fields, and rode home with him on his horse. Melchor Clemente had a horse to ride because he was the foreman.

Roberto ran down the road. He ran past the men in their large straw hats, wearily carrying the machetes that they used to cut the cane.

Soon he saw his father astride his big brown horse. "Papa! Papa!" he called. His father saw Roberto running to meet him. He leaned down from his saddle and put out his arm to help Roberto up onto the horse. Roberto took his father's hand and climbed up behind him.

Roberto put his arms around his father's waist and they started down the dusty road. Roberto loved to ride the horse home with his father. When they reached their house, he slid down and then his father dismounted. He helped his father take the saddle off, lead the horse to the small corral, and close the gate.

José was still in the field batting at the tin cans. He was throwing them up in the air and hitting them. "Roberto, come play ball!" he called.

Roberto looked at his father for permission. Melchor Clemente nodded. "You can play for a while, but be sure to come when you are called for dinner."

Roberto's father went into the house. He was very hot and tired from his long day of hard work in the sugarcane field. He was glad to wash up in the cool, fresh water and to sit down as Roberto's mother cooked the evening meal for the family.

Roberto ran over to where José was standing with his broomstick bat over his shoulder. He picked up a can and tossed it to José. He swung and hit it. Roberto tossed another can and again José hit it. Then he missed, and it was Roberto's turn to hit. José threw can after can to Roberto, and he hit the cans all over the field!

It was José's turn at bat again when Roberto's older sister Rosa called him.

"Momen [pronounced Momay], come in for supper."

José was disappointed. "Do you have to go? We won't have time for you to pitch the cans for me to hit."

"We can play after dinner. I'll pitch to you," promised Roberto.

"Momen!" Rosa called again.

Roberto dropped the can he was holding. "I've got to go now." He started across the road.

José asked, "Why does your sister call you Momen?"

Roberto laughed. "She just does. I *am* Momen." And then he said, "I'll be out to play after I've eaten."

Roberto ran across the road to his house. He was very proud of his house and his family. Although they did not have much money, their wooden house was bigger than most of the houses in their barrio. The big front porch kept the sun from beating into the rest of the house, and breezes blew through the open windows. They had a living room, a dining room, a kitchen, and five bedrooms. They also had an indoor bathroom, which most of the other houses did not have.

"Come to eat," called his mother as she set out the rice and beans on the table for the children to eat. His father sat down in a big chair by the open window in the living room. In most Puerto Rican families, the father was served his food first and then the mother would serve the children.

Oswaldo said, "Papa should eat first. We should wait. He has worked hard all day in the fields."

"Come, Papa, for your supper," Rosa said. "We will wait." She looked at the food on the table. "Maybe there won't be enough."

Melchor Clemente smiled as he looked at his wife. They believed in feeding the children first, then eating what was left. "No, this is what your mother and I choose. Because of the war, sometimes food is hard to get. We want you to have enough food to eat, so that you will grow strong. There will be plenty for us to eat when you have finished. Now eat your mother's good food."

Roberto did not understand about the war. It did not seem to have anything to do with Puerto Rico, but his mother and father said the United States was at war with Germany and Japan. German submarines lurked unseen in the waters along the coast of their island, so it was difficult for Puerto Rico to ship the sugar to the United States to sell. And the foods that Puerto Ricans needed could not be shipped onto the island.

Roberto's family laughed and talked as they ate. The older boys talked about playing baseball after their supper. Roberto asked, "May I play, too?"

His father laughed. "That's all Roberto wants to do . . . bat a ball around!"

"We don't need to worry whether he has enough food," his mother replied. "He'd rather play ball than eat."

Roberto smiled shyly and looked down at his plate. He didn't say anything. He just hoped his big brothers were going to play ball this evening and that they would let him play with them.

"Come on, Momen. We're going down to the Barrio San Anton School to play in the kids' league," said Matino.

"Can José come, too?" asked Roberto. "I promised to play with him after supper."

"Of course—we were planning on him playing, too."

"Who else is playing?" asked their father.

"Everyone," answered Andres. "José will be there, Cousin Lorenzo, and several others."

"Aren't they all much older than Roberto?" asked their father. "He's only eight."

"Sure, but don't worry about Momen," Matino answered. "He plays as well as most of the big kids. He was born to play baseball!"

José was waiting in the field across the road with all the tin cans when Roberto and his brothers started down the road to the field by the schoolhouse.

"Come on, José," Roberto said, waving to him. "We're going to play at the school-house."

Roberto and his brother Oswaldo ran down the road to catch up with Matino and Andres. "Wait for me!" José called.

Roberto stopped by the side of the road and waited for José while Oswaldo went on to

the field. When Roberto and José arrived, most of the kids were already there. The bigger kids had bats made from guava trees, gloves made from coffee bean sacks, and a ball made of tightly wound rags.

Though the sun was sinking in the west, its rays, as they slanted through the palm and bamboo trees, were still hot. The air was quiet and warm and moist. The boys ran to take their places on the field. They were ready for a fast and exciting game.

All of the Clemente boys were great ballplayers. Matino usually played first base, and he almost always put the runners out with his amazing catches. And when Matino didn't catch the ball, Andres would. He would throw it in with his strong arm, which always found its mark. When Lorenzo came up to bat, he hit so hard that the ball of rags flew up onto the roof of the schoolhouse.

Roberto looked so small and thin as he came up to bat. But when he swung his bat he connected with that ragged ball and sent it flying. He ran as fast as he could to first base. His brothers were certainly glad to have him on their team! But no matter which team won, all of the kids had a good time, and played as hard as they could.

Working in the Fields

ROBERTO AWAKENED EARLY. He could hear the dogs barking and the roosters crowing. He was excited because his father had said that he could go with him to the sugarcane fields today. The shutters were still closed for the night, so he didn't know whether it was time to get up yet. Then, with a thud, his father threw open the shutters, letting the bright sunshine into the room. Roberto hopped out of bed and ran out on the porch, where he could see the shutters opening on all the houses up and down the street. The sky was blue, and the fresh morning air was moist and cool and filled with the fragrance of bougainvillea flowers and jasmine. Roberto thought their barrio must be the most beautiful place in the world in the early morning.

Roberto's mother made breakfast and coffee. After his father had eaten, he got ready to go to the sugar fields. He took two cords, which had come from the bags of beans and rice, and tied them tightly around his ankles.

"Roberto, take these and tie them around the legs of your pants." He handed two cords to his son. Roberto did as he was told. He knew it was important to have your pants legs tied tightly around your ankles to protect against insects and snakes. All of the cane cutters in the fields tied the cuffs of their pants legs.

Melchor Clemente got his machete and said, "Come on, Roberto." Then he picked up the coffee, water and bread that Roberto's mother had packed for them to take to the field. As they walked out the door he put on his broad-brimmed straw hat. "Be sure to get your hat, son," he said. "You will need it in the hot sun."

Roberto felt like a big man going with his father. He opened the gate and took the horse out. One of his brothers had already saddled the horse for them. His father placed the food and machete in a bag and swung himself up into the saddle. Then he helped Roberto up onto the horse behind him and they set off down the road to the fields. Other men and boys walking to the sugar-cane fields joined them on the road.

The sun was climbing high in the sky, and by the time they got into the fields, sweat was already beading up under Roberto's shirt. Roberto liked the smell of the cane, which grew all around their village like a forest. As they walked into the field, the stalks of sugarcane towered nearly fifteen feet over their heads. The men formed cutting lines, and with sure, swift strokes, they swung at the stalks with their sharp machetes. After they cut the stalks very close to the ground, they chopped the leaves off, cut the stalks into halves or thirds, and dropped them on the ground. The cane was collected in piles and then gathered up and placed on carts to be taken to the factory.

Roberto helped by picking up the cane and putting it in piles. His father made sure that he was far enough behind the cutters and their swinging machetes that he would not be in danger of getting hurt. Señor Clemente supervised his crew of cutters, and he also cut cane with his sharp machete. The cutters formed a long line as they moved against the cane, and it fell before them as they cut.

It was very hot in the sugarcane field. The tall cane cut off any breeze and heat came up

from the ground, so it felt like being in a stove. Roberto's entire body was wet with sweat. He could feel it running down his face into his eyes. He tried to rub the sweat with the back of his hand, but the rough scratchy hair of the cane scraped his face. He wiped behind his neck, and the fuzzy, rough hair of the cane went all down his back.

Roberto felt he was doing well and working hard, but he was relieved when his father finally told him they could stop and take a break to eat. It was nine o'clock and the whole line of workers put their machetes down where they were and got out their breakfasts. They needed to eat in order to have enough strength to work until noon. They sprawled on the ground covered with the cut cane and rested their tired arms and legs as they ate.

Melchor Clemente looked at his son with pride. Even though he was small, he had worked right along with the other boys and men without complaint. Señor Clemente poured a cup of water for Roberto and gave him a thick piece of bread spread with margarine before starting on his own coffee and bread. They didn't talk. They just rested and ate.

Roberto looked about him. They were surrounded by the tall cane, with the path of cut cane behind him. The men had loaded the cane on wagons which would be driven to the factory to be made into sugar. His father took a piece of cane from the ground and with his machete deftly cut off a small piece and handed it to him. Roberto took it happily and chewed and sucked the sweet stalk.

After a short break, the work continued. The men called it "doing battle" with the cane. And it was something like a battle, as the men charged forward, chopping down the forest of cane before them. The day grew hotter and hotter, with the blistering sun shining down on the thick field of sugarcane.

Señora Clemente brought their dinner to them at noon. She had been cooking all morning. She carried a big wire rack from which pots hung, filled with food. One pot was full of rice and another of red beans in a tasty sauce. A third pot contained boiled green bananas, taro, and yams. All of the men working in the sugarcane fields had hot meals at noon brought to them by their families.

Roberto was glad to sit down to eat. As he and his father ate their rice and beans, Melchor told his son a little of the history of the island. He told him that they were descended from the *Jibaros*, who were a proud people native to Puerto Rico. The *Jibaros* had come down from the mountains years ago to work in the cane fields. They always worked hard and took care of others who needed help.

He went on to tell Roberto that Christopher Columbus had come to the island in 1493. The Spanish took over the island and Ponce de León was the first Spanish governor. The Spanish ruled the island for many years, and that was the reason the language of Puerto Rico was Spanish.

"Did the Spanish play baseball?" asked Roberto.

His father threw back his head and laughed. "No, at least as far as I know. The Americans took Puerto Rico from the Spanish in the Spanish-American War of 1898. When the American army came here, they played baseball. But long before that the Indians of Puerto Rico played a game which was very much like baseball. They played on fields bounded by rows of flat stone. They wore heavy stone belts, which they used to hit a rubberlike ball through a stone ring."

Roberto thought about how it would have been to try to hit a ball with a heavy stone belt. He frowned as he thought of more and more questions. "Is Puerto Rico part of the United States?"

His father nodded, "Yes, and we are citizens of the United States."

As they were talking, Don Pepito, who was the owner of the Rupert Brothers Sugar Company, drove through the fields on his way to San Juan. It was about a fourteen-mile trip from Carolina to San Juan, and almost half of the journey was through his own fields. He drove past the workers, resting in the fields they had just leveled. Don Pepito glanced to the left and right at the men who worked for him. The owner of the sugar company looked very dignified sitting in the backseat of his car as his chauffeur drove him through the hot fields on his way to lunch in a cool restaurant in San Juan. He waved to the workers as he passed, and nodded to Melchor Clemente, because he was the foreman. Roberto felt proud as his father, standing straight and strong, nodded his head stiffly in return. His father watched the car as it passed.

"Remember, Roberto," he said, "Don Pepito is no better than you!"

The Special Surprise

THE LONG DAY in the sugarcane field finally came to an end. At four o'clock, with the hot sun still beating down on the fields, the workers stopped slashing at the cane with their sharp knives and started the walk back to their homes.

Roberto took his hat off and wiped the sweat from his face and head. He was glad that his father had brought him to the fields to work, but he was even more glad that the day was over. Melchor Clemente sat straight and tall in the saddle, and

Roberto climbed up to sit behind him.

On the way home, Roberto and his father passed a group of boys playing baseball. Roberto noticed they were using a real rubber ball, not a tin can. He thought about how much he wished he had a real rubber ball, too.

Almost as if his father knew what he was thinking, he said, "Roberto, I haven't seen you playing with your rubber ball. What has happened to it?"

"It finally wore out," Roberto answered. "It came apart in little pieces."

His father smiled. The house was quieter when Roberto didn't have a ball to bounce against the ceiling and the walls, but he knew how much Roberto wanted one.

They continued the ride home in silence. Roberto was almost too tired to talk. He wished he could get another rubber ball that he could bounce, but he didn't want to ask.

After Roberto slid off the horse, his father

dismounted and they put the horse away. His father turned to him.

"I have a few pennies that you can have to buy another ball," he said.

Roberto was so pleased and so surprised! "Thank you, Papa," he said with appreciation as he took the pennies and started to run down the road to the little store. Suddenly, he didn't feel so tired.

"Wait," his father stopped him. "First, we will wash up and have our supper. Then you can go get your ball."

Roberto washed his hands and face as quickly as he could. His mother was already serving food for the family to eat. On this night they had a pot of delicious pork to go along with their rice and beans. Roberto sat down and started to eat. He was really hungry, but he was also eager to go down to the store to get a ball. He hadn't had a real ball for a long time.

His brothers had all been working, too.

Matino had been loading the truck. The other two had been working in the fields, loading the sugarcane onto the carts which took it to the factory to be made into sugar. They were all very hungry.

Roberto finished his supper first. "May I be excused?" he asked.

Matino looked up. "What's your hurry? You don't usually finish your supper before the rest of us."

"I am going to get a new rubber ball," Roberto said.

"Are you going to play ball tonight?" Andres asked.

Roberto really wanted to, but he was so tired he ached all over.

His mother answered for him. "No ballplaying for Roberto tonight. He has worked too hard today. He needs to rest."

"I'll rest after I get my new ball," said Roberto, getting up from the table. "I'll be right back." He ran out the door, letting it slam behind him. He hopped off the porch and headed down the street toward the little store.

He ran past some of the women in the neighborhood. They were taking down their clean clothes from clotheslines, which were strung from their houses to nearby trees. Young children were playing in the yards around the small houses. Goats were ambling about in the street. As he went along, one old goat, his whiskers bobbing up and down as he chewed, kept getting in his way. Roberto laughed at the funny animal as he good-naturedly shoved the goat out of his way.

Some of his friends were playing in the water at the standpipe and asked him if he would like to join them. They were splashing each other and slipping and sliding in the mud around the pipe. The water looked cool and inviting, but Roberto was eager to get his rubber ball. "Not now," he answered. "I am getting a new rubber ball at the store, and then I have to go home." He was very tired after his day in the cane field.

When he reached the little store, he climbed up the wooden steps and went in. He carefully selected a little, round, spongy rubber ball, then handed his pennies to the storekeeper. Roberto felt so lucky to be able to have a real rubber ball. He walked back down the street to his house as fast as his tired legs would go. "Look, Mama," he said as he entered the kitchen. "My new rubber ball."

"Well, isn't that nice," his mother said, smiling and shaking her head. She was not really very happy about this. When Roberto had a ball, the whole house thudded from his throwing it against the wall.

Roberto went in and lay on his bed and bounced the rubber ball. He bounced it against the wall and then bounced it against the ceiling. Every once in a while, he would just squeeze it in his hand to make his hand

and arm stronger. He thought about all the men in the cane fields and how strong their arms were from swinging their machetes.

As he lay bouncing the rubber ball against the wall, his eyes started to close. Finally, he had one of his rare misses as he fell asleep.

Slam! Roberto awakened with a start when he heard the front door close. "What was that?" he exclaimed, sitting straight up in bed.

"That was Mama leaving, as she does almost every night," Oswaldo, who shared a room with Roberto, answered sleepily. "She is going to Don Pepito's house to do their laundry."

Roberto lay back down again. He remembered that his mother woke up at one o'clock in the morning to go to Don Pepito's house and do their laundry. She did it at night so she could be home during the day for her family. Roberto felt so tired. He thought about how tired his mother must be going to work in the middle of the night after she had worked so hard all day.

They all worked hard. When the boys were not in school, they worked in the sugarcane fields with their father during the harvest. This started in November and lasted until early summer. Rosa worked in the house with their mother, helping with the cooking and the laundry.

From mid-summer to November there was no work in the cane fields. All the people in the neighborhood had to stretch their money to feed their families and pay their bills. They grew food in their gardens and ate fruit from the trees. Sometimes, if they had friends who were fishermen, they could get some fish or turtle meat.

During this time when there was no work in the fields, Melchor Clemente and his sons would work with their truck. They used the truck to haul sand or construction material. Señor Clemente also used the truck to deliver food from the Clemente's store to the people in the barrio. Sometimes his neighbors did not have money to pay, but he always gave them the food. He kept a record of the food he had sold, and his neighbors would pay what they owed once they went back at work in the sugarcane fields. Melchor Clemente felt it was important to help people who were not as fortunate as he.

Everyone in the Barrio of San Anton was relieved when November rolled around again. It was the beginning of the working season in the sugarcane fields, so there was money for everyone again. People no longer had to worry about getting food and paying their bills.

November was also important for another reason: It marked the beginning of the winter baseball season in Puerto Rico. The San Juan Senadores played baseball at Sixto Escobar Stadium. After the men came home from work, they would gather on the street and talk about the baseball games. They talked about who had played well and who had not. They decided how the manager should have played the game. When the boys played baseball in the lot across from Roberto's house, they also talked about the real baseball games and who was winning. That made November a very special time for Roberto.

One evening, Roberto noticed that some of the boys who played ball had bicycles. They would ride up to the field, lay their bicycles down by the road, and then run to the field to play.

Roberto wished he had a bicycle. Then, when they played games in other fields, he, too, could ride to them on his bike. He thought about how nice it would be to be able to ride wherever he wanted to go.

He planned how he would ask his father. He would list the reasons why he needed a bicycle. First, with a bike, he could do errands for his parents. Second, riding a bicycle would make his legs strong. Third, he could . . . well, he couldn't think of any other good reasons, except that he wanted a bicycle.

One night after supper, instead of running across to the field to play ball, he sat in the living room bouncing his ball against the wall. "Please, Roberto," his mother said, "that is enough for now. Take your ball and go outside."

He stopped bouncing the ball, but he sat waiting for his parents to finish their supper. After what seemed like a very long time, his mother got up to clear the table. She saw Roberto still sitting in the living room. "It is very strange that you are not out playing ball," she said. "You must want something. Are you still hungry? Do you want something more to eat?"

Roberto shook his head no. He had been waiting to talk to his father. "Papa, can I get a bicycle?" he asked.

"If you want a bicycle," his father answered, "you will need to earn the money for it."

Roberto knew that was fair, but he wondered how he could earn that much money. He thought about what kind of work he could do. But he couldn't think of anything. Then, a few days later, he heard that their neighbor, Señora Ruiz, was having trouble getting her milk from the store. It was a half mile away. Roberto thought he could get her milk for her!

Señora Ruiz told him that she would pay him a penny a day if he would take her empty milk can to the store each morning and have it filled with milk. He was delighted!

The next morning at six o'clock Roberto stopped at Señora Ruiz's house to pick up the big milk can, then started off with it to the store. He walked down the road with the men who were setting out for the sugarcane fields. Early mornings felt so good. The air

was cool. The red flowers bloomed all around the houses. The shutters on the houses were opened, and the delicious smell of coffee mixed with the sweet fragrance of the flowers.

The storekeeper filled the big milk can and Roberto picked it up with both his hands. He was surprised that the can was so heavy, but Roberto was strong and thinking about the bicycle he was going to buy gave him incentive. When he placed the can inside the front door, Señora Ruiz came out to pay him. She thanked him and carefully placed a shiny penny in his hand.

He ran home with his earnings. His mother got down a glass jar from the shelf over the stove, and Roberto dropped his penny in the jar. Each morning he went for the milk and delivered it to the neighbor's house. And each day he dropped his penny in the glass jar. He knew that with each penny, he was a little bit closer to having his very own bicycle!

Ten Home Runs!

ONE DAY AFTER Roberto added his penny to his savings, his mother put the glass jar back on the shelf and said, "Roberto, eat your breakfast and get ready for school. Your brothers have already finished eating and are ready to leave."

He ate his breakfast quickly, washed his hands and face, and ran out the door to catch up with his brothers and his friends on their way to school. Roberto and his friends went to the Fernandez Grammar School, which was near the Clemente house, just on the other side of a group of banana trees.

On their way to school, José and Roberto picked up some old bottle caps from the trash along the side of the road. When they got to the school yard, Roberto picked up a guava stick from the ground.

"José, toss me some bottle caps," he said.

Roberto swatted away at the bottle caps that José pitched to him. After he had hit them all, he and José went around picking them all up. They were stacking all of the caps in a neat pile at the base of a tree when the teacher rang the school bell. They ran into school. They didn't want to be late.

The morning at school seemed very long. All the windows in Roberto's schoolroom were open. Even though it was wintertime, the weather was still warm. As Roberto sat studying his spelling words, he looked out the window at the blue sky. He watched the long fronds of the palm trees dip and sway in the breeze. It wasn't easy to keep his attention on the words in front of him.

The teacher smiled a little. She could see the girls and boys laboring on their schoolwork. She could tell they wanted to go outside and play. Looking up at the clock, she was glad to see that it was almost time for recess.

"You may put your work away now and get ready for recess. We'll have our spelling test review when we come back afterward."

Roberto put his spelling book in his desk. Then he carefully took his rubber ball out and held it in his hand. He held onto it tightly because he didn't want it to roll away and have the teacher take it away from him.

The bell rang, and the children all ran out the door and onto the dusty playground. The girls ran to play under the banana trees, and the boys snatched up their guava bats and went to the field to play ball.

They ran and took their places in the field. Roberto grabbed a bat, ran to home plate, and stood ready to hit the ball. He tossed his small rubber ball to José, who was going to pitch to him. José threw the ball and it went very low. Roberto jumped back to try to hit it, but just barely tapped it. He scooped the ball up from where it had rolled and tossed it back to José.

José threw the ball again. Roberto hit it right on, but it didn't go very far. The rubber ball was too soft and too small.

"Here, use this!" one of the other boys shouted. He tossed a ball of rags wound tightly together to José.

Roberto got his rubber ball and laid it by the schoolroom door to take inside with him when recess was over.

"Come on, Roberto, step up to the plate if you're going to hit!" called Guillermo.

"Okay, throw the ball!" Roberto answered. He stood with his bat ready.

José stood straight, just like the real pitchers did at the Senadores games. Quickly he tossed the hard rag ball at Roberto.

Roberto was standing with his legs apart, ready for the pitch. When the ball came toward him, he swung and hit it squarely. All of the boys playing turned their heads to watch the ball fly through the air. It came down just before it hit the tops of the banana trees.

Roberto ran to first base and then to second before Manuel got the ball and threw it back to José.

The other boys took their turns at bat. Some of them hit the ball and some missed.

There were not enough boys playing to make two teams, so they just all took turns at bat and in the field. They enjoyed playing this way, and were disappointed when the teacher rang the bell because recess was over.

Roberto had a hard time keeping his mind on learning the spelling words, and he couldn't wait until it was time to go home for lunch. Finally the bell rang. As Roberto ran out of school, he saw his mother. She was returning home after having taken Roberto's father his lunch, and was carrying the metal rack with the pots hanging from it. "Mama, let me help," he said, running up to her. He took one end of the rack.

"Thank you, Momen," she said. The two walked along together on the road, past the banana trees and into their house. Inside, Roberto's mother placed the pots back on the stove. Then she dipped up some hot noodle soup from one of the pots and set out some cornmeal cakes for Roberto. As Roberto ate, he bounced his ball on the floor and thought about the baseball game after school.

"Mama, there is going to be an important ball game right after school," he said seriously.

His mother laughed. "They are all important! You may play ball, but bring your books home from school first."

"I'll have to hurry, or they will start without me."

Doña Luisa smiled. "I am sure you will be

able to play whenever you get there. And now stop bouncing your ball and eat your lunch so that you can get back to school on time."

The hot afternoon went slowly for Roberto, but at last school was out and he ran home. He left his books and the little rubber ball. Then he went down to the playing field by the school, where the boys were already gathering.

Most of the boys were much older than he was, but they were glad to have him on their team. Roberto always tried harder than anyone else, whether he was hitting or trying to catch the ball and put another player out. His amazing skill at baseball was already becoming apparent.

The first time Roberto came up to bat, Pedro was pitching. Roberto leaned forward, swung the bat, and sent the ball straight into the trees. He dropped his bat and ran to first. The boys were still scrambling to find the ball, so he dashed on to second. Then he kept on running past third and on to home!

"A home run for our side!" Andres shouted.

They played the entire afternoon, with Roberto getting hit after hit! The boys were having so much fun, they didn't even know what time it was.

Roberto was up at bat again, and hit another solid home run. As he ran around the bases he saw his father and some of the other workers standing by the field watching the game.

They were on their way home from work. They were hot, dirty, and tired, but they were so interested in the ball game, they had stopped to watch. Señor Clemente was very proud of Roberto as he made hit after hit. He asked how many home runs Roberto had.

"He has hit eight!" Manuel shouted.

Another boy came up to bat and struck out. The next boy hit the ball, but was thrown out at first. This happened over and over again. The hitter either struck out or was put out at first.

Roberto came up to bat again. The pitcher tried to make it hard for him by throwing balls which were almost impossible to hit.

He let the first two pitches go by, and then swatted the third one with a mighty whack that sent the ball flying. By the time the fielders got to the ball, Roberto had charged clear around the bases for another home run!

The game was almost over, and the men, tired as they were, had to stay until the end to see what would happen.

One other batter got as far as second before he was put out. And then Roberto came to bat again and hit his tenth home run of the game!

Roberto's father and the other men cheered. They just couldn't help it. It was such a good hit, and *another* home run!

When they got home, Roberto slumped in his chair at the kitchen table. He was so tired he could hardly lift his fork to eat the food in front of him.

"Do you feel all right, Momen?" asked his mother when she saw that he was not eating.

"I'm okay," Roberto nodded. "I'm just tired."

"Tired! It's no wonder he's tired!" Roberto's father exclaimed. "Roberto played some ball game today. Everyone else just stood around while Roberto kept running around the bases! The other boys didn't have to run. They stepped up to the plate, and either struck out and didn't run at all, or, if they did get a hit, they were put out at first. But Roberto got a home run almost every time he came up to bat. He had ten home runs in the game!"

Pennies in a Jar

AFTER NEARLY THREE years of dropping the pennies in the glass jar from any work Roberto had done, it was almost full. Roberto asked his mother if he could count the money. With her strong arms, she lifted the heavy jar from the shelf and placed it on the kitchen table.

"There is a bicycle for sale, and I hope I have enough money to pay for it," Roberto told his mother. "Papa went to look at it to see if it's in good shape."

"How much does the bicycle cost?" asked his mother.

At that moment Roberto's father arrived home, and came striding into the kitchen. Señora Clemente turned to look at him as he answered her question. "The young man who is selling the bicycle would like thirty dollars for it, but he might take a little less."

Roberto had changed some of his pennies for dollar bills, but the jar was still heavy. He counted his money carefully as his mother and father watched. They looked at each other and smiled. They were proud that Roberto had worked so hard and for such a long time in order to save his money for something he really wanted.

At last Roberto finished counting. He had twenty-seven dollars!

Matino came into the kitchen. When he saw Roberto's pile of money on the table, he teased, "Oh, good, I need some money. Can I borrow some?"

And then Andres and Oswaldo came in, and they each teased their younger brother, asking to borrow money. They knew how long he had worked and saved for a bicycle.

"Come on, Roberto," their father said, putting an end to the teasing. "Let's go talk to Señor Gonzalez to see if we have enough money to buy the bicycle."

"Shall I bring the money along?"

His father nodded. Roberto got a thick rice sack and poured his money in it. Then he and his father walked down the road to see if they could buy the bicycle.

After they had left, Matino asked, "Do you think they can buy the bike for twenty-seven dollars?"

"I think so," Andres answered confidently. "Señor Gonzalez is a big boss at the sugar factory, and the bike belongs to his son, who now wants to buy a car."

And he was right, for it was not very long before Roberto came riding up on his very own shiny blue bicycle! Andres and Matino went out to the road to admire the new

bike, and they all took turns riding it.

Roberto was very proud of his new bicycle, and he was glad to share it with his brothers and his friends. Though he liked to ride the bike, for the most part he rode it only to the fields to play baseball.

Every night the house was filled with the sounds of the rubber ball bouncing against the walls and the ceiling. Roberto would lie on his bed, bouncing the ball, with his ear close to the radio. He would listen to the baseball games at Sixto Escobar Stadium in San Juan. He hung on to the announcer's every word. He could imagine the game as it was being played.

Because the weather was warm all year in Puerto Rico, baseball could be played throughout the winter months. Many of the big league stars from the United States would come to the island to play during the winter season in the Puerto Rican Winter League.

Roberto listened to as many games as he

could. He followed all the players, but most of all Monte Irvin. He was one of the stars of the Negro National League in the States and played for the San Juan Senadores in the Puerto Rican Winter League.

"José," Roberto called one day as he ran across the field to play ball, "did you hear the game last night?"

José nodded his head. "Sure." Most of the boys listened to the games on the radio.

"Did you hear what Monte Irvin did?" Roberto asked. Without waiting for José's answer, he went on. "He slammed two home runs! And then he made a great catch on a ball that was almost out of the park —"

José finished the sentence for him. "That won the game for the Senadores!"

"And then . . . and then . . . he threw Juarez out at first," Roberto continued. "He sure has a great arm."

Roberto idolized Monte Irvin not only because he was a terrific hitter, but also because he was such a good fielder. He would frequently pick up balls in the outfield and throw runners out at first! Roberto talked about Monte Irvin so much that sometimes his friends teased him and called him Monte.

Roberto was ready to play wherever he saw a baseball game. He had a tattered baseball glove that was always hanging on the handlebars of his bike and an old bat which he carried with him wherever he went.

One afternoon, his mother sent him to the store to get a package of needles and some sewing thread. He hung the small bag on his handlebars as he started back home. The store was only a half mile or so from his house, but on his way he noticed that his friends were playing ball. He got off his bicycle to watch. He meant to stay for only a few minutes. But one of the boys called, "Momen, come take a turn at bat!"

Roberto dropped his bike and grabbed his bat and glove. He ran to home plate, dropped his glove on the ground, and swung his bat over his shoulder, ready for the pitch. Pedro was pitching, but on this afternoon he couldn't hit the side of a barn with his pitches. Try as he might, Roberto couldn't reach the ball to get a hit. He was disgusted.

He grabbed his old glove and went to the outfield. He ran all over the field, making amazing catches. Then, finally, he came up to bat again. This time he was determined to get a hit.

On the first pitch, the ball went high and outside of home plate. Roberto reached, swung his bat, and connected. The ragged ball went flying into the trees at the edge of the muddy field. Roberto ran and made it all the way around for a home run. "Run, Monte, run!" José yelled.

The boys played and played. Finally, they had one of the other boys pitch, and Roberto got another good, solid hit! He made it all the way to third base this time.

The sunlight was almost gone, and the dusky gray of evening settled over the field, but Roberto didn't even notice. Suddenly, one of the boys noticed how dark it was getting.

"I've got to go home," he said.

Roberto looked about and realized it was late. For the first time since he had started playing, he remembered the things he was supposed to take home to his mother. "Oh, no!" he said. "I've got to go, too!"

He grabbed his bat and glove, picked up the little package, and hopped on his bike. As he rode along he realized it was later than he thought. There weren't any men on their way home from work; everyone was already home for supper. When Roberto pulled up in front of his house, he could see that the family had finished supper and only his mother was in the kitchen.

Doña Luisa looked at him, all sweaty and

dirty from his baseball game, with his tattered baseball glove and bat. His feet were muddy, and his shirt was smeared with dirt.

Doña Luisa was very angry! Her eyebrows were drawn into a deep frown, and her mouth was straight and tight.

"All you think of is baseball!" she said crossly. She grabbed the bat from him and threw it into the fire of the cookstove!

Roberto couldn't believe it! His mother was always so patient and calm. He was horrified as he saw his bat begin to burn. He rushed to the stove and snatched it from the flames, then threw an old empty rice sack over it. His hands were hot as he pounded on the sack until all the sparks were out. Luckily, he had gotten the bat out before it was too badly burnt.

"I'm sorry I was late. . . . I didn't mean to be!" he cried to his mother. He felt bad that he had been so late; he knew he was wrong.

His mother took a deep breath. "I'm sorry,

too. . . . But you spend too much time on baseball. You need to get an education so you can go on to college and become an engineer."

Roberto's mother wanted him to be an engineer, not a baseball player. But Roberto knew that he was born to play baseball. Years later, when Roberto was grown and a professional ballplayer, his mother often said that she had made a mistake that day, and that he was right to have wanted to play.

A Trip to the Barber

ROBERTO'S HAIR WAS thick and curly, and it was hard for him to comb, so he didn't. But his mother decided it was time that Roberto's hair was combed.

"Sit down here," she said, pointing to a chair. She held the comb in her hand.

"Do I have to?" Roberto resisted.

"Yes, I am going to comb your hair." She took the comb and tried to pull it through his hair. He tried to wiggle away from her. "Sit still!" she said.

"Ouch, it hurts," Roberto complained.

His father came in as his mother was trying to comb his hair. He watched the battle his wife was having with Roberto's hair. "I don't know why Roberto doesn't comb his hair himself," he said.

"I know why," Señora Clemente replied. "It's too hard to get a comb through his thick, matted hair."

"Then I'll take him to the barbershop," said his father. Roberto and his father went down to Hector Fidalgo's barbershop on Calle Domingo Caceres. As father and son marched in, Melchor Clemente said, "Cut it short!"

The barber Fidalgo tried to comb through Roberto's hair in order to cut it, but he broke his comb. The pieces of the comb clattered on the floor as they fell. He then took another comb from his table, and it broke, too! Then another! With disgust, he strode out of the shop saying, "Wait! I'll be right back!"

He went to the hardware store and bought

a steel comb which was made to be used on horses, and returned to his shop. Roberto winced as the barber pulled the comb through his hair. Then, with his sharp scissors, Fidalgo chopped most of it off. When he had finished, he said, "Roberto, do not come to my shop again!"

Strangely enough, years later, after the World Series of 1960, Roberto walked into a barbershop in Rio Piedras in San Juan and there was Fidalgo the barber! Fidalgo was very glad to see Roberto, who had become a famous baseball player.

After Roberto's haircut, his head was still hurting from having his hair pulled so hard, but not so much that he wasn't ready to play baseball. He got his bat and glove and ran to the ball field as soon as he and his father got home.

The boys teased him because of his new haircut. Some of the boys also asked what had happened to his bat, which looked a little

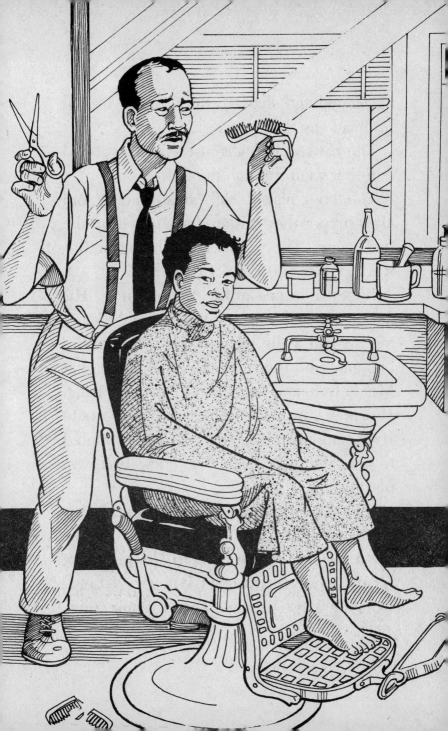

blackened and charred. Roberto just turned his head and didn't answer.

The bat still hit balls just as well as it had before it went through the fire.

The boys played ball all afternoon, and after supper they gathered again to continue their game. They didn't stop playing until it was too dark outside to see the ball.

Roberto came in for the evening. His father watched him go into his room, bouncing his ball as he went. Then he heard the ball game on the radio. He could hear that Monte Irvin and the Senadores were playing. He knew how much Roberto idolized Monte Irvin, and how much Roberto always wanted to hear the games when he knew Irvin was playing.

Irvin was named the Most Valuable Player of the 1946 Puerto Rican Winter League. Then, when he went back to Newark, New Jersey, he was the named the Negro National League's Most Valuable Player. Later in his career, he played with the major league New York Giants and briefly with the Chicago Cubs.

As he was listening to Roberto's radio, Don Melchor decided to give Roberto the opportunity to go to Sixto Escobar Stadium. He knew if he gave him bus fare to go down to San Juan to buy lottery tickets, Roberto would get to see Monte Irvin play.

The bus went past Sixto Escobar Stadium, where the Winter League baseball games were played, on the way to San Juan. He knew that Roberto would get off the bus at the stadium and peek in through the fence at the game for a while. He would stand and watch, and then walk the rest of the way to San Juan, nearly a mile farther. Then he would buy the lottery ticket for his father, get back on a bus, and go home.

A few days later, when he knew the Senadores were playing, Melchor Clemente called Roberto from his ball game in the field across the road. Roberto dropped his bat and ran to see what his father wanted.

"Would you want to go into San Juan to buy a lottery ticket for me?" his father asked.

Want to! He could hardly wait! He knew that the Senadores were playing. "Oh, yes," he replied quickly.

Don Melchor handed Roberto money for the lottery ticket and ten cents for the bus, which cost five cents each way.

Roberto was so happy! He ran back to get his bat and called to his friends, "I can't play any longer now. I'm going into San Juan."

He brought his bat back home and put it on the porch, then ran down to the bus stop.

He'd waited for only a short while before the big bus pulled up and stopped, its brakes creaking. He climbed on the bus and rode along on the bumpy road almost all the way into San Juan. He watched carefully, and when he saw the stadium, he signaled the driver to stop.

He hopped off the bus and ran over to the fence. He tried to see through, but there were people inside the ballpark blocking his view. So he walked farther on to reach another spot by the fence where he could see.

Roberto saw Monte Irvin come up to bat. He could feel his heart pounding as Monte stepped up to the plate. He almost felt as if he himself were standing there. He watched as the ball was pitched and Monte swung. But Monte only got a piece of it, and the foul ball came flying out of the park. It went over the fence right where Roberto was standing! He ran as fast as he could to get it. He was so afraid someone else would get there first!

As he scooped up the ball in his hands, he couldn't believe his good luck! If there had not been people blocking his view, he would not have moved, and he would not have been where the ball landed.

He clutched the ball in both his hands as he walked on into San Juan. He couldn't believe that he had gotten a ball which Monte Irvin had hit! He held on to the ball carefully as he bought the lottery ticket and got on the bus to return home.

When he got home, he had to tell his brothers about his wonderful find! He wouldn't part with the ball. He let them see it and hold it, but when he went to bed he took it with him and slept with it.

The next day Matino asked if they could play with the ball. It would be great to be able to play with a real baseball, Matino explained. Though Roberto found it difficult to part with the ball, he didn't want to be selfish, and so he let his big brothers have it for their game. He played, too. He felt so special when he came up to bat. He was about to hit the same ball that Monte Irvin had hit!

As they were playing, the skies suddenly darkened and the heavens opened with a lashing rainstorm. The players ran as fast as they could to take shelter under some palm trees, but they were drenched from the downpour before they could get there.

The warm rain ran down their faces, and their clothes were soaked through. Roberto clutched his ball to his chest, trying to keep it dry.

The storm didn't last long, and when the sun came out the boys went back to play on the muddy field. Roberto didn't want to use his ball anymore, but the older boys really liked playing with a real baseball.

Everything seemed to be fine until Oswaldo came up to bat. He got a hit that sent the ball straight into a ditchful of water. Not just any ditch, either, but the one some hogs used as a mud wallow!

Roberto ran to the muddy water and fished the ball out. He ran home and went to the standpipe by the side of the road. He washed and washed the ball until it was clean again. Then he went in and asked his mother if he could have an old rice or bean sack to dry it with.

Though Doña Luisa got tired of all the baseball games and the bouncing balls, she could understand why this ball was so important to Roberto. She got a sack and handed it to him. He took it and wiped the ball very carefully to get it totally dry, then took the ball into his room to keep it safe.

Melchor Clemente watched as Roberto placed the ball under his pillow. Then the boy turned on the radio, tuned in to the baseball game at Sixto Escobar Stadium, and lay down on his bed. He could hear the crowd yelling and cheering as Monte Irvin came up to bat.

As the announcer described the game, he could see his hero swinging the bats, choosing one, and then stepping up to the batter's box, still swinging the bat in his strong, muscular arms. Roberto listened as the announcer talked about what the pitcher was doing and then said loudly, "Here comes the pitch!"

Roberto listened intently for the hit, but Irvin let it go by. "Ball one!" called the umpire. On the second pitch, Monte Irvin swung his bat and hit the ball with a mighty crack! The crowd roared. Roberto's chest filled with excitement, and he yelled, "All right!"

Roberto's father was sitting at the kitchen table and heard Roberto's shout. He laughed. He knew how much Roberto admired Monte Irvin. He looked at the coins in his little cash box and made a decision.

"I Am Roberto Clemente"

WHEN ROBERTO CAME into the kitchen the next morning for breakfast, his father was getting ready to go to the fields for work. He looked up as Roberto entered, and asked, "Are the Senadores playing today?"

Roberto answered, "Yes."

"Is Monte Irvin playing?"

"Yes, he is playing." He wondered at his father's questions.

Melchor Clemente stood up straight and took a quarter from his pocket. Roberto thought this was strange because his father never carried money in his pocket when he was going to work. "I happen to have a little extra money today. You may take this and go to the ball game today."

Roberto could not believe his ears! "Thank you!" He didn't know what else he could say to show how grateful he was.

He didn't need to say anything else. Don Melchor knew how much Roberto appreciated being able to go to the game. He looked at Doña Luisa, who was working at the cookstove. She smiled her approval. Though she felt school was much more important than baseball, she was happy that Roberto would get to go to a game.

Roberto could think of nothing else as he sat in school. He wanted to tell his friends, but he didn't want to seem boastful. As soon as the teacher rang the final bell, he ran home to drop off his schoolbooks.

He got the quarter, which he had carefully placed in his dresser drawer, and ran to catch the bus. He climbed on the bus and gave the driver the five-cent fare. He kept five cents for the ride home, and he had fifteen cents left over for a bleacher seat.

The bus rumbled along the dusty road into San Juan. When it reached Sixto Escobar Stadium, Roberto hopped off and ran to get in line to buy his ticket.

With his ticket held tightly in his hand, he hurried to the bleachers. He climbed up and up to find somewhere to sit. He sat down and looked around at all the other people at the ball game. Though the sun was very hot, the strong fresh breeze from the sea was cooling.

The game was exciting, and Monte Irvin was just great! Roberto held his breath each time Monte came to bat. He watched his every move as he swung the bat over his shoulder and stood ready for the pitch. He moved with perfect timing as he hit the ball, slugging it almost to the fence. Roberto leaped to his feet and cheered along with the other fans.

Then he watched with admiration as Monte fielded the ball with his strong arm and threw out several opposing players. To add to Roberto's excitement, the Senadores won the game! It was no wonder that Irvin had been voted the Most Valuable Player in the Puerto Rican Winter League.

Roberto sat on his bench in the bleachers as the fans filed out of the park. He didn't want his day at the ball game to be over. He watched as the teams left the field and went to their locker rooms. Then suddenly he thought that maybe he could see the players, and especially Monte Irvin, if he went down to the locker room door and waited for them to come out.

He ran down the stairs of the bleachers and hurried to the locker room door. He thought about how much he would like to say something to Irvin, but he knew he could never be bold enough for that. He just wanted to see him.

Several of the players walked out, and finally Monte Irvin came through the door. Roberto didn't have the courage to look directly at him. He dropped his gaze. After Irvin had passed, Roberto looked up at him as he walked away. He couldn't believe his hero had just walked by!

Roberto would always remember seeing Monte Irvin playing baseball, and standing so close to him for a moment that he could have touched him. As Roberto played ball, sometimes he would think about how Irvin hit and how he threw, and he would try his very best to be like him.

After Roberto completed elementary school, he went to the Julio Vizcarrondo High School in Carolina.

Roberto was a good student, but he was shy and usually sat in the back row of his classes. Señora Marie Caceres, his history teacher, was very kind to him and recognized that Roberto was a good student, even though he did not speak out much.

All of the classes were taught in English, and it was not always easy for Roberto to understand what was being said. He spoke Spanish. He had learned only a little English in elementary school. So he did not raise his hand to be called on very often.

Though it was difficult for Roberto to master English in his classes, it was easy for him to excel in sports.

Some of Roberto's friends who knew how fast he ran in baseball games said, "Why don't you come out for track-and-field with us?"

And so he did, and he was one of the squad's fastest runners. He practiced jumping and he learned to throw the javelin. The track coach was pleased that he had such a real winner.

Roberto loved all sports, but he loved base-ball most of all, and felt that the skills he was developing in track-and-field would only make him a better baseball player.

Roberto studied hard and helped with the work at home, but he still played ball every minute that he could. One evening in 1948, when he was fourteen years old, Roberto was playing ball with a group of his friends on the dusty sandlot. They were using tin soup cans for balls and a broomstick for a bat. They were playing the same game they had played so often, where one person bats and everyone else fields, and if a batter strikes out, he has to pitch. Roberto never had to pitch because he never missed.

A man strolled up to the field and watched the game for a while. His name was Roberto Marin, he was a salesman for the Sello Rojo Rice Company, and he had a softball team. He would walk around the sandlots to find players for his team. He watched for a while as different boys came to bat. Some of the boys were hitting well, but there were several

who struck out. Most of the boys he had seen were playing all right, but they were not good enough for his team.

Then Roberto came to bat. Señor Marin watched Roberto swing at the first can and send it flying to the end of the field. And then he saw Roberto hit the next can, and the next, and the next. The cans were flying all over the field. Marin was amazed at this boy who never missed. He called over to him, "What is your name?"

Roberto answered, "I am Roberto Clemente."

Without hesitation, Marin said, "Come to Carolina tomorrow and try out for our softball team."

The Very First Uniform

ROBERTO LISTENED AS Señor Marin told about the tryouts the next day. He went home slowly, thinking about playing on the softball team. He told his father about Marin's invitation and asked him if it would be all right for him to try out.

"There is nothing to be lost by trying," Melchor Clemente said as he nodded his permission. "I give you my blessing."

After school the next day, Roberto jumped onto his bicycle to ride the short distance into Carolina to try out for the team. As he rode his bicycle up to the fence, he saw a group of players on the field. They all looked much bigger and older than he was. He wondered whether he was at the right place. Then he saw Señor Marin, who called to him.

"Come over here and let's see you hit."

Roberto dropped his bicycle and walked to the plate. He picked up the bat that was lying there and waited for the pitcher to throw the ball.

Señor Marin tried to encourage him, saying, "Don't worry, you'll hit just fine."

Roberto said nothing as he waited for the pitch. He wasn't worried—he knew he would hit just fine. And, of course, he did!

After seeing Roberto hit every ball pitched to him with the same power as he had hit the soup cans, Señor Marin chose Roberto to play on his Sello Rojo Rice softball team. He gave Roberto his very first uniform: a red and white T-shirt with the letters of the team on it.

In the beginning, he played shortstop. Then Marin put him in the outfield, and he excelled there. He ran fast enough to get under almost every ball hit anywhere near him. As he leaped to make the catch, oftentimes his cap would fall off, and the fans would cheer and cheer! For the first time, Roberto was playing real ball games in front of real crowds, and he loved it!

When he was only fourteen he was selected to compete in the 'future stars' competition, where most of the other boys were sixteen years old.

Señor Marin was very proud of the way Roberto played. Never had he seen a boy who loved baseball the way Roberto did.

Roberto spent all his spare time playing and practicing. He always carried the rubber ball around with him, and would squeeze it to make his hand and arm stronger. After the games the team would go out for something to eat and drink. But

Roberto always drank milk and then went straight home to bed.

Though he continued playing for Roberto Marin's Sello Rojo Rice softball team, Roberto also began to play hardball for the Ferdinand Juncos team in the Puerto Rican amateur league in 1950, when he was sixteen. These players were on a level of play with the Class A minors in the U.S. professional leagues.

Roberto also became a star on his high school track-and-field team. He was named the Most Valuable Player on the team. He triple-jumped an outstanding forty-five feet and high-jumped six feet.

Some of his teammates wanted him to enter the 440-yard race, but Roberto said, "I'm not good enough to compete in that event."

"Sure you are," his friends said.

"If the coach wants me to run I will, but there is no way I could win against the good runners in the 440-yard race," Roberto replied.

His friends insisted that he try. They knew he could win, only Roberto thought he was not fast enough. But Roberto decided to run, and, as always, did his very best.

Roberto ran the 440-yard race and beat a couple of boys thought to be the two fastest runners on the island! Then with his strong right arm he threw the javelin 195 feet!

Some who saw Roberto's wondrous track-and-field accomplishments felt he should try out for the Olympics team. But Roberto was really not that interested in track-and-field or the Olympics—he wanted to play baseball.

Señor Marin agreed with Roberto that he should play baseball. Though Roberto was only eighteen, Marin felt that he was as good as many of the professional ballplayers from the United States who participated in the Puerto Rican Winter League.

Pedrin Zorilla, the owner of the Santurce

Crabbers, one of the top baseball clubs in the Winter League, was a friend of Roberto Marin's. Marin felt that Señor Zorilla should know about Roberto Clemente.

One day Roberto was walking back to the bench after the Sello Rojo Rice team had just won a game. Señor Marin came along to walk beside him, and said, "I'm going to talk to Pedrin Zorilla about you."

Roberto was still excited over the catch he had just made that had ended the game. He knew that Señor Marin was pleased with his team's winning season, but he couldn't understood why he would want to tell Pedrin Zorilla about him. He frowned a little as he said, "Pedrin Zorilla about me?"

"You know the Santurce Crabbers Baseball Team?" said Marin.

Of course Roberto knew the Crabbers. He had followed their games on the radio. "Sure I know the Crabbers . . . they are a great team!"

"Pedrin Zorilla is the owner of the Crabbers and he also does some scouting for the Brooklyn Dodgers," Marin explained.

Roberto nodded. He recognized the name of Pedrin Zorilla and knew he was a very important man.

Marin continued. "Of course, you know that the Crabbers are one of the best teams in the Winter League. Señor Zorilla has many fine players on his Crabbers—some of them even come from the States to play on his team." Roberto knew about the ballplayers from the States who played here in the winter, like his idol, Monte Irvin.

"I think he might be interested in your ballplaying." Marin said. And he walked away, leaving Roberto standing there. Roberto's eyes widened and his heart pounded. He didn't know exactly what Roberto Marin meant. Did he think Señor Zorilla might consider him to play for the Crabbers?

Roberto Marin visited Pedrin Zorilla and

was received with courteous hospitality. Señor Zorilla wondered about the purpose of Marin's visit as they talked about the weather, which was very hot, and the baseball season.

Zorilla politely asked Marin about the Sello Rojo Rice team, and how its season was going. "The team is doing very well. We have some very good young players this year," Marin replied. He hesitated and then went on. "There is one very talented young ballplayer I would like to talk to you about."

Señor Zorilla smiled to himself as he recognized the real reason for Marin's visit.

"I think you might be interested in him." Then, Roberto Marin added with emphasis, "This boy is meant to play baseball!"

Zorilla listened politely, but if he was interested in Roberto, he didn't show it.

He was used to signing players who were professionals and had been playing for a long time. Through the years, he had signed some of the best baseball players from the States to play on his teams. He wasn't interested in a very young player who had only played on small local teams.

Often friends told him about young players, most of whom were not really ready for professional baseball. Also, if he seemed too interested, even if the young player was very talented, he might think he was worth too much money.

Marin could see that Señor Zorilla did not believe Roberto was any different from other young players. He leaned forward and said, "Pedrin, you need to see Roberto Clemente play."

Señor Zorilla said dryly, "I am sure he is a fine ballplayer."

"He's plays on my softball team, and at the same time he plays with the Ferdinand Juncos team," Roberto Marin went on. His voice grew a little louder with his enthusiasm. "He is truly an exceptional player. He can hit balls all over the field, and he is an outstanding outfielder. He chases after everything. In my opinion, he is as good as any of the professional players who come down here to play ball!"

The expression on Señor Zorilla's face didn't change. He shrugged his shoulders. He had heard about young, inexperienced players before, but to satisfy Marin he said, "Okay, tell Roberto to come to the tryouts which the Crabbers and the Dodgers are holding next week at Sixto Escobar Stadium."

Al Campanis was going to be there from the Dodgers, though, like Señor Zorilla, he didn't usually expect to find players who were good enough for the major leagues.

Tryouts

AL CAMPANIS, SCOUT for the Brooklyn Dodgers, held the tryout camp at Sixto Escobar Stadium. Roberto Clemente was surprised as he looked around at the large group of boys who had turned out.

Al Campanis was not surprised. Whenever he held tryouts for the Dodgers, many boys would come to try their luck, but it was rare that any of them were good enough to make it. These were youngsters with dreams, and Campanis was glad to give them their chance, but he didn't often find real ballplayers.

There were seventy-two boys in center field to take the first of the tests, which was making a throw to home plate from center field.

Campanis watched as teenager after teenager stepped up to throw. Some of the balls went far awry of home plate. Some balls were thrown so slowly that a good runner would easily have taken an extra base. Some throws went too high and others didn't make it all the way. It was hard for Campanis to pay attention. There were so many boys, but none came close to the level of skill that Campanis was looking for.

Then came Roberto's turn. Campanis was hardly watching any longer when suddenly he heard the loud smack of a ball hitting a catcher's mitt. He turned to see what had happened. He saw Roberto, a serious, slim boy in a T-shirt with a baseball cap pushed back on his head.

Campanis shouted to him, *"Uno mas!* Once more!"

Roberto hesitated for only a moment and then he threw another fast ball straight into the catcher's mitt. Campanis couldn't believe what he had just seen! Again he called, "*Uno mas*! Once more!"

And again Roberto's throw was perfect: fast, straight, and directly into the catcher's mitt!

Campanis felt like the tryouts had finally come to life! He started the group on the next test, the sixty-yard dash. Roberto led all others. Campanis had timed the race and, according to his watch, Roberto had run the 60 yards in just 6.4 seconds. At that time the world record for the dash was 6.1 seconds. Roberto had run nearly as fast as the runner who held the world record!

The Dodger scout could not believe that this young boy had run that fast, though clearly he had run faster than any of the others. He had to see him run again. "*Uno mas*! Once more!" he called.

Campanis set his stopwatch, and clicked it

as Roberto started to run. With his strong legs flying, Roberto streaked past. When the scout stopped his watch as Roberto reached the end, he saw that Roberto had again run the 60 yards in just 6.4 seconds!

"Thank you all for coming. Tryouts are now over," Campanis called out to the young players.

Roberto had slowly started to walk out of the park with the others when Campanis called him back. "Go on over there . . . pick up a bat and hit a few for me." He pointed to the batter's box, and went over to stand behind the cage to watch. He thought to himself, If this boy can hit at all, we need to sign him to a contract to play ball.

Roberto picked out a bat and stood waiting for the pitch. The pitcher was one of the Dodgers' minor league pitchers. Campanis watched as Roberto hit line drives all over the field, one after another, for nearly twenty minutes! He noticed the way Roberto was

standing and told the pitcher to pitch him a ball outside. He didn't think Roberto could reach a pitch there. To Campanis's complete amazement, Roberto swung with both feet off the ground and hit strong line drives to the right and ground balls up the middle!

Campanis thought Roberto Clemente was the greatest natural athlete he had ever seen. He would have liked to sign him for the Brooklyn Dodgers right then and there, but he knew he would have to wait a year because of a major league rule that said that a player could not be signed until he'd graduated from high school. And Roberto still had one more year to go.

The Puerto Rican League, however, did not have this rule. On the following Sunday, Pedrin Zorilla went to see a Juncos game. He had not been at the tryouts, though Campanis had told him just how good Roberto was. Roberto hit balls surely and truly to get on base, ran too fast to be put out, made two catches in center field which looked impossible, and threw out a runner at home plate!

He was every bit as good as Roberto Marin and Campanis had said! When he saw how well Roberto played, Zorilla offered him a four hundred dollar bonus and forty-five dollars a month to play with the Santurce Crabbers.

Zorilla took the contract to Roberto's father. Melchor Clemente, who could not read or write, took the paper to a neighbor who could read it. Roberto was so excited he could hardly stand still. He stood on one foot and then the other as the neighbor put on his glasses and slowly read the contract.

The neighbor said, "If Zorilla wants him badly enough to pay him four hundred dollars, maybe he would pay him much more."

Don Melchor was thoughtful. "Do you think so?"

"Papa, are we going to take the contract

back to Señor Zorilla?" Roberto asked anxiously. He was tremendously eager to play ball with the Crabbers.

"Yes, let's go," Melchor answered.

Roberto Marin went with Melchor Clemente and Roberto. When Don Melchor looked around at Señor Zorilla's elegant house and fine furnishings, he thought that perhaps his neighbor was right and that Señor Zorilla would pay Roberto more money. So Don Melchor asked Señor Zorilla how much more he would pay for Roberto.

Zorilla was very firm. "That is my final offer."

Marin nodded, and took Roberto and his father aside. "This is a good offer. Not many rookies start out with a four-hundred-dollar bonus."

Roberto was anxious; he didn't want to lose this chance. He said, "I will do whatever you say! I just want to play ball!"

Melchor Clemente saw how much

Roberto wanted this opportunity, and he said to Señor Marin, "Tell the man I will sign for Roberto!"

On October 9, 1952, the contract was signed for Roberto Clemente to play professional ball with the Santurce Crabbers, *Sangrejeros* in Spanish. Señor Zorilla also got Roberto a new glove when he saw his torn, beat-up one.

Roberto was very excited to be playing real baseball with real professional players, but his excitement soon turned to disappointment. Pedrin Zorilla's policy on young players was for them to learn by watching, not by playing. He felt that coming up against older pros could make a young player unsure of his own skills.

But Roberto did not agree with this policy and was becoming angry. He asked his friend Roberto Marin, "Why am I not playing? I don't understand!"

Marin encouraged him, as he was to do many times during Clemente's career. "Just be patient. Your time will come."

And come it did. Before the end of the 1952–53 season, Roberto was in the regular lineup. Buster Clarkson, the team manager, recognized what a fine baseball player Roberto would become, and gave him both encouragement and help in improving his skills.

Clarkson watched as Roberto batted, and he could see where Roberto needed to improvement. "Roberto, you are dragging your left foot when you swing," he told him.

He placed a bat behind the boy's left foot so he couldn't drag his foot when he batted. He was a patient man, but he was especially so with Roberto because he realized what great potential Roberto had.

Finally, Buster Clarkson knew he had to give him his chance. Although the team had three other good outfielders, Clarkson gave

him the opportunity to play. There was no doubt he belonged in the regular lineup!

Clemente started the 1953–54 season with the Santurce Crabbers as the regular right fielder. He played so well against the professional ballplayers that before the season was out, many of the scouts from major league teams were looking at him.

The Big Leagues

BEFORE THE END of the 1954 winter season, the Brooklyn Dodgers offered Roberto a ten thousand dollar bonus and five thousand dollars in salary. Roberto and his parents were amazed at the size of the offer. Other teams were also bidding, but the Dodgers offered the most. Besides, the Brooklyn Dodgers were a famous team and Roberto wanted to play for them. It was easy for him to decide to take their offer.

However, a short time after he announced that he had accepted the Dodgers' offer, he received another offer for an unbelievable amount of money. He was approached by a scout from the Milwaukee Braves who offered him a bonus of thirty-five thousand dollars to sign a contract with them. Roberto didn't know what to do. He had told the Dodgers he would accept their offer, but thirty-five thousand dollars was an enormous amount of money!

He sat at the kitchen table with his mother, attempting to think through his decision. Her face was calm, and she said nothing as she watched Roberto trying to decide. Finally he looked at his mother and said in a worried tone, "I don't know what to do! I gave the Dodgers my word, and we shook hands on the agreement, but I haven't signed a contract yet." He took a deep breath. "But thirty-five thousand dollars is so much money! What shall I do?"

Doña Luisa didn't hesitate as she answered firmly and clearly, "When you give your word, you keep your word!"

So, on February 19, 1954, nineteen-year-old Roberto and his father signed the contract with the Brooklyn Dodgers, which Pedrin Zorilla sent to the United States.

In the spring of 1954, the Dodgers sent Roberto Clemente to play with their top minor league club, the Montreal Royals. His father went with him to the airport. The day was sunny and warm, and the breezes blew through the palm trees. Roberto was excited, but he felt lonely as he thought about leaving all his family and friends. His father bid him good-bye. "Take care of yourself, Momen. Buy yourself a car, and don't depend on anyone else."

Roberto climbed up the steps to the plane, then turned to wave good-bye to his father. Despite his joy at going to play baseball in the big leagues, for a moment he had a sad feeling in his chest.

When he arrived in Montreal, he was nearly

two thousand miles from home in a strange land with a strange language. Leaving the airport, he looked up at the gray sky, and shivered as the chilly air went through his light jacket.

As he made his way to his hotel room, he was surprised to hear only French being spoken. At the baseball park, English was the language spoken, but when he was in Montreal—going to the room where he stayed, or taking buses, or doing anything— the language not only wasn't his familiar Spanish, it also wasn't English, which at least he knew a little. It was French, which he did not understand at all!

He felt a little more comfortable when he was playing ball; then, he knew the language of the game. He could talk to and understand his fellow players with his poor English. But when he left the ballpark and needed to take a bus, the bus driver spoke only French. He would try to watch carefully so that he could get off the bus at the corner near the hotel. He thought about his father's advice to get a car and not depend on anyone else. That would help with his getting where he wanted to go, he knew, but it would not solve all his problems with the language.

One evening he went into a little restaurant to get something to eat. A very pleasant waitress brought him a menu, but he couldn't read it because it was all in French.

When the waitress returned, Roberto said, "I would like some chicken with rice and beans."

The young lady's face was blank. She didn't understand.

Roberto felt so homesick. He looked out the window of the little restaurant, and saw thin white snowflakes tumbling down. It was spring! And it was snowing! His thoughts turned to the warm breezes and bright sunlight of his homeland. Then he remembered that he was hungry. He decided that after this maybe he would just have to eat hot dogs at the ballpark. And he didn't even like hot dogs!

He looked around. There was a man at a table behind him eating some kind of meat and noodles. He pointed and said, "I'd like that."

The waitress smiled with relief that she could understand what he wanted, and went to get his order.

The food was hot and tasted all right, though not like his mother's good cooking. But he felt better after he had eaten. He walked to his lonely room and went to sleep, just waiting until tomorrow when he could go back to the ballpark.

Unfortunately, his days at the ballpark with the Montreal Royals were not much better. Max Macon, the manager of the Royals, kept Roberto on the bench more than he let him play. Roberto could not understand why. When he played badly, Macon let him play.

When he played well, he benched him. Why would the Dodgers pay him all that money and then not let him play? Roberto was very discouraged.

In one game early on, he had swatted a home run four hundred feet away, well over the left field wall of the Royals' stadium. He was happy that now the team would see what he could do, and he would be able to play more. But the next day he was on the bench!

Another time he was in for the entire game and hit three triples. He was benched for the next two games.

Finally Roberto called his friend Roberto Marin and said, "I am going to quit!"

Marin, again, encouraged Roberto, saying, "Take it easy—you're just starting. It will be okay."

Roberto did stay, but he was on the bench for nearly all of the last twenty-five games. Later he figured it out—the Dodgers were trying to hide him because they didn't want any of the other major league teams to know how good he was.

At that time, the rules were that another team could draft a player who had received a bonus of more than four thousand dollars and was not playing on the major league team. But that was exactly what happened, despite the Dodgers' attempt to hide Clemente.

The Pittsburgh Pirates, because they were in last place, had the first draft choice, and they were watching Roberto Clemente.

Clemente first came to their attention when Clyde Sukeforth, a Pirates scout, went to look at Joe Black, a Montreal pitcher. He just happened to see Clemente practicing throws before the game. And after that, he only had eyes for Roberto.

Later Roberto was a pinch hitter in the game, and Sukeforth was impressed with his hitting. When Sukeforth found out that

Roberto would be available in the draft, he went back to Pittsburgh and told Branch Rickey, the general manager for the Pirates, about this talented young player.

Late in the regular season, Howie Haak, another Pirates scout, came to see Clemente. Max Macon heard that Haak was there, and so he called Clemente back to the bench and would not let him hit.

Of course, Roberto did not yet know why he was being pulled from games, and he was furious. He went back to his room at the hotel and started jamming his clothes into his suitcases. He was going to go back to Puerto Rico. He had had enough of the Montreal Royals!

Suddenly there was a loud knocking at his door, "It's Howie Haak of the Pirates."

"Go away, I'm on my way to Puerto Rico," Roberto shouted.

Oh no, thought Haak. If Clemente left now, before the start of the International

League playoffs, the playoffs for the AAA farm system, he would not be allowed to play on any major league team! No one was allowed to just quit a team or one of its affiliates. Walking out at that moment would mean Roberto would be blacklisted for the rest of the year, possibly longer.

"Please let me in," called Haak.

Roberto opened the door, but he continued packing.

Haak talked as fast as he could, which was difficult because his Spanish was so poor. "If you leave now, you will be on the ineligible list—then no one can pick you in the draft!" He pleaded, "Roberto, finish the season first, and then go home. If you do, I promise you, next year you'll be playing every day for the Pirates!"

A New Beginning

ROBERTO UNPACKED HIS bags and finished the season with the Montreal Royals. Then, just as Howie Haak had promised, on November 22, 1954, the Pittsburgh Pirates made Roberto Clemente their first draft choice. They got Clemente from the Dodgers for four thousand dollars. Clemente was glad to be done with his season with the Montreal Royals and to be going to a club where he could play—despite the fact that he didn't even know where Pittsburgh was!

Roberto returned to Puerto Rico after his

disappointing season in Montreal. Roberto was very happy to be back home, but he was worried about his brother Oswaldo, who was very ill. Then, one day as he was going to visit his brother, another car struck his. Roberto received a severe back injury, which caused him pain off and on for the rest of his life.

But in spite of his injury, after he recovered, Roberto played the 1954–55 winter season with the Santurce Crabbers. He was glad to be back among players he understood. The team had a great season, and Roberto played exceptionally well.

Pedrin Zorilla had gotten Willie Mays, who had the highest average in the National League in 1954, to play with the Crabbers in the 1954–55 season. Though Mays was four years older than Roberto and had a few years of major league experience, Roberto played almost as well as he did. There was very little difference between them.

But Roberto still liked to watch Mays to

see how he could improve. He watched Mays catch fly balls, and studied his swing. Willie Mays was also very helpful. He told Roberto, "Don't let the pitchers get to you. Just get up there and hit the ball. Show *them!*"

Years later, a sports announcer, thinking that he was complimenting Roberto, said, "You play ball like Willie Mays."

"Nevertheless, I play like Roberto Clemente!" Roberto quickly retorted.

In the spring of 1955, Roberto reported to the Pittsburgh Pirates, who had been finishing last in the National League year after year. Proudly, he put on his uniform, emblazoned with the number 21. Roberto brought honor to the number for the next eighteen years!

As Haak had predicted, Clemente did not have to sit on the bench. He got to play! After his experience in Montreal he was fiercely determined to play well and win. The Pittsburgh Pirates fans fell in love with this enthusiastic young player with the great fielding skills and the strong right arm. Pirates play-by-play announcer Bob Prince called Roberto "Arriba." The fans chanted "Arriba! Arriba!"

Unfortunately, no matter how well he played, the Pirates continued to lose. But whether the team was winning or losing, Roberto always played his best.

When he was angry, he played all the harder against the other team. Sometimes he would become so angry and disappointed at all the lost games, he'd take his anger out on the plastic batting helmets. One time, when the Pirates lost again, he threw down his helmet and kicked it as far as he could. As the losses piled up, he not only kicked his own helmet, but slammed and crushed other helmets with his bat.

After he had done this several times, Fred Haney, the manager, came to him and said, "If you want to destroy your own things, that's up to you." Then he squared his shoulders and looked Roberto in the eye. "But if you want to smash helmets, it will cost you ten dollars a helmet."

Roberto looked at the mass of shattered plastic helmets and counted twenty-two of them beaten into bits. He knew that translated to $220. He knew he didn't have money to waste that way. It was the last time he took out his anger on helmets.

He loved being at the baseball field, and he spent hours practicing, but he was homesick in this northern city. His English was still not very good, and he could not understand the racial prejudice against him, both as a black and a Puerto Rican. Most of Pittsburgh's black people lived in one section of town, called the Hill. He had two black teammates on the Pirates, and they told him, "Just don't pay any attention to the insults; keep still and ignore them."

Roberto could not accept the abuse. His parents had brought him up to respect other people, and that respect had nothing to do with color. He had to speak out when he felt he, or anyone else, was being treated unfairly.

His one good friend in Pittsburgh was Phil Dorsey, a postal worker who knew the city well. He found a place for Roberto to live with friends, Stanley Garland and his wife. Stanley also worked at the post office and had just built a new house. The Garlands became almost like parents to Roberto.

Phil and Roberto spent a lot of time together. They went to the movies together, or watched TV, and Phil helped him with his English. Phil Dorsey was always a good, trustworthy friend to Roberto.

It was difficult for Roberto to return to spring training in Florida in 1956. The black players on the team had to stay in a different hotel from the rest of the team. Oftentimes, the team went into restaurants where they wouldn't serve Roberto and his black team-mates. This made Roberto very angry. He had never known this kind of treatment before he came to the States.

During the 1956 season, Clemente fielded incredibly and threw as he always had. In the ninth inning of a game against the Cubs, with two outs and the score tied 8–8, Roberto was running the bases as fast as he could. When he got to third, coach Bobby Bragan signaled him to stop, but Roberto yelled, "Get out of my way and I score!" He ran on, slid into home plate in a cloud of dust, and Pittsburgh beat the Cubs 9–8!

Roberto admitted after the game that he had deliberately run through the coach's stop signal. He'd said to himself, We have nothing to lose. The score is tied without my run, and if I score the game is over and we won't have to play anymore tonight!

Roberto's back hurt, and oftentimes he did not feel well. He also had many other injuries. Danny Murtaugh, who became the team's manager in 1957, often seemed not to believe that Roberto was sick or hurt. This really upset Roberto. He knew he always played when he could, and played his best. Roberto complained when he didn't feel well, but then he would go out on the field and play a spectacular game. The sportswriters and many others used to say that he could play better when he was sick than other players could when they were well!

Each winter season, Roberto returned to Puerto Rico. He played winter baseball and spent time with his parents and his family. He bought a new home for his mother and father. One of his friends said, "It is so good for you to give a home to your parents."

Roberto said, "I'm not giving them something! I'm paying them back for giving me so much!"

In 1957, Roberto spent the six months he was not playing with the Pirates serving in the Marine Corps Reserves. He was stationed at the Marine boot camp at Parris Island, South Carolina. All of the physical training helped his back, and when he reported for spring training, he was feeling strong and healthy.

In each of the three years before Clemente started playing with the Pirates, they had lost more than 100 games. Five years after he joined the team, in 1960, the Pittsburgh Pirates won the World Series against the New York Yankees!

In United States baseball there are two major leagues, the American and the National. The teams in the American League compete against each other to win the pennant for being the best team in the American League. The teams in the National League compete for their pennant.

The two winners then play against each other in the World Series to decide the World Champion. The winner has to win four games out of seven.

In that pennant-winning season, Roberto Clemente batted .314, with 16 homers, 89 runs scored, and a team-high 94 runs batted in.

Clemente always played his very best. In one game that year at Forbes Field in Pittsburgh, Willie Mays hit a ball down the right field line. Roberto had to catch it! He ran as hard as he could, caught the ball, and ran into a concrete abutment. Blood gushed from his injured jaw, but he held on to the ball to maintain his teammates' shutout. He held up the ball so the umpire would know that the catch had been made. The fans went crazy, shouting, "Arriba! Arriba!"

He was taken to the hospital to have his chin stitched up and wasn't released until five days later. During those five days, the Pittsburgh Pirates' seven-game lead in the pennant race dwindled down to only two games. When Roberto got out of the hospital he went back to play immediately. The

Pirates went on to win the pennant, their first in thirty-three years! Then they went on to face the New York Yankees in the World Series.

The New York Yankees were an almost unbeatable team, but the Pittsburgh Pirates were ready for the challenge. Roberto said, "I had to remember to hit to right field."

He remembered. The Pittsburgh Pirates fans chanted, "Arriba! Arriba!" as he hit safely in all seven games.

Roberto celebrated with his team in the locker room, but after a short time he went outside to celebrate with the fans. He said, "I feel like one of them. I've never seen anything like them. I wanted to be with the people who pay my salary." And the fans loved him right back!

Roberto was very disappointed when he was not voted the Most Valuable Player for the year by the sportswriters. He may not have expected to win the award against teammate Dick Groat, who did receive it, but he was really insulted when he found out that he'd come in eighth in the voting!

Publicly he said, "I didn't receive the recognition I felt was due me. I felt I had a very good year and I also felt that it was overlooked." This hurt lessened his joy in winning the World Series.

Dreams Coming True

DESPITE ROBERTO'S FINE playing, Manager Danny Murtaugh was very skeptical about his injuries and illnesses. Roberto had two operations on his elbow. He also suffered an injured ankle in an accident on the field, and his back hurt him much of the time. On more than one occasion, Murtaugh accused Roberto of not being too sick to play. Roberto knew that he always played unless he was so sick that he could not, and he resented Murtaugh's not believing that.

For the most part, the sportswriters did

not give Clemente the credit he deserved that year. But the Pittsburgh Pirates fans cared nothing about where the sportswriters placed him in their voting or what the manager thought about Clemente's injuries.

The fans loved Clemente and knew how hard he played for them. Whenever he got up to bat or came out on the field, they chanted, "Arriba! Arriba!" They felt extremely close to him, not only when he was playing for them, but when he would stand for hours signing autographs. And the love was mutual; Roberto felt very close to his fans.

He always had time to talk to youngsters at the ballpark. He said he felt proud when kids asked for his autograph. One time, at a ball game in Houston, he was introduced to a deaf teenager in the stands. Roberto talked with him for a while using his hands and smiles.

A short time later, he returned with one of his bats. He climbed up fifteen rows in the grandstand and gave it to the deaf boy. On the bat he had written, "Jamie, you don't have to be able to hear to play baseball and enjoy the game. Best wishes, Roberto Clemente."

During the 1961 season Clemente was consistently the best hitter and the best right fielder in the National League. Clemente led the hitters in the league batting race by finishing the season at .351, and he had a career- and league-high 27 assists to win the National League's Gold Glove Award for being the best fielder at his position. And, in August of 1961, in a game against Cincinnati, Clemente got his 1,000th career base hit.

Roberto learned to control his anger when pitchers threw balls at him to make him step back or to hit him. He also kept his concentration after he had two strikes, and would frequently get base hits in that situation. In one game, he got base hits five times after he had two strikes!

Opposing pitchers could not figure out how to throw a ball he could not hit. The way he stood in the batter's box, it looked as if he couldn't hit an inside pitch. But he could, and did! And the way he moved, it looked as if he couldn't hit on the outside half of the plate. But he did! Murtaugh was never skeptical about his talent, saying, "Just name one thing he can't do. There's nobody better!"

In 1961 the players, coaches, and managers voted Roberto Clemente to the National League All-Star team for the All-Star Game at San Francisco's Candlestick Park. Roberto hit a triple and batted in two runs, including the winning run in the bottom of the tenth inning. Danny Murtaugh, who coached the All-Star team, kept him in for the whole game. Roberto felt good that Murtaugh had left him in for the entire game, because it is customary in the All-Star contests to play each of the players for only a part of the game so that everyone has an opportunity to shine.

After his team's win, Roberto was proud to wear the 1961 All-Star Game ring.

On October 9, 1961, a huge celebration was held in San Juan when Roberto and San Francisco Giants' star Orlando Cepeda returned home. Their fans were honoring Roberto's 1961 batting championship and Orlando Cepeda's many home runs and RBIs. They were the first players from Puerto Rico to ever lead in any of the three main batting statistics in the major leagues. They were met by eighteen thousand cheering fans at the airport and along the route of their motorcade to Sixto Escobar Stadium.

These were very good years for Roberto. In 1962 he was again named to the All-Star team, and again in 1963.

After the 1963 season was over, Roberto returned to Puerto Rico as he always did in the wintertime. One sunny November day he went down to Oscar Landrau's drugstore, and his life changed forever.

Oscar Landrau had stepped out of the drugstore for a few minutes. So Roberto sat down and began reading the newspaper.

The door opened, and in stepped the most beautiful young lady he had ever seen. She was tall and graceful as she walked over to the prescription counter. She stood at the counter for a few moments, and she looked puzzled as she waited for Señor Landrau.

Roberto was watching her every move. She glanced around the store. He looked over the top of his newspaper and said, "He'll be right back."

She smiled, but did not answer, as she continued to stand at the counter.

Roberto wanted to say something more. He wanted to ask her her name, but he knew that was not proper.

A minute later, Oscar returned. After

making her purchase, the tall, beautiful girl turned and went out the door.

Roberto went up to Oscar at once and asked, "Who is that girl? What is her name?"

The pharmacist smiled. "Her name is Vera Cristina Zabala, but her parents are very strict and you dare not speak to her unless you are properly introduced."

Roberto felt as if he were floating on air. "Mama, I am going to get married," he said when he got home.

"You are going to do what?" Doña Luisa couldn't believe what she was hearing.

"I have just seen the girl I am going to marry."

Roberto set about trying to arrange a meeting with Vera. He learned that she also lived in Carolina, not too far from his house, and that she worked at the Government Development Bank.

Without stopping to think that in Puerto Rico a young man did not just call up a girl without having been properly introduced, he called Vera at the bank. He sent her flowers. He wanted to ask her to lunch.

Vera would not answer his phone call. Her parents, she knew, would never allow her to go out with a young man she didn't know.

One day he did get through to Vera. He asked her to lunch, but she very politely refused.

Roberto talked with Señora Marie Caceres, his high school teacher. He asked her if she knew Vera. She replied, "Of course—Vera was one of my best students. You can't just call her up to talk to her."

"What can I do? I have to meet her!" Roberto replied.

Gently Señora Caceres said, "Do you remember Mercedes Velasquez?"

"Oh yes, of course."

"I believe she is a friend of Vera's."

Roberto stepped up his quest to meet Vera. He called Mercedes Velasquez every day, trying to arrange an introduction. Finally Mercedes planned a small party and Roberto just "dropped in."

Vera knew very little about baseball, and did not know that Roberto was a professional baseball star. He invited her to go to a game. The Crabbers were playing at Hiram Bithorn Stadium in San Juan. Her parents permitted her to go, as long as her sister Anna Marie and another couple went along as chaperons. Roberto wanted her to see him play baseball, but his plan was spoiled, because the game was rained out!

He was disappointed about the game, but he said, "Let's go to a nice restaurant for dinner."

Then he was really disappointed when Vera and Anna Marie said that they couldn't go. Their parents had given them permission only to go to the baseball game, not to go out to dinner!

Vera's parents were very proper. Even though she'd attended the University of

Puerto Rico and had a responsible job in a bank, she still needed to ask her parents' permission even to walk down to the corner.

But Vera had begun to like Roberto. In an old-fashioned type of courtship, they had dates through the winter, and by the time Roberto reported for spring training, they were engaged.

The year 1964 was a spectacular one for Roberto, who was named to the All-Star team once more. He won the batting title again. He played in 155 games, and had a batting average of .339. He had 211 hits, tops in the majors. He scored 95 runs and drove in 87 for his strongest showing since 1961.

And then his dream came true when he and Vera Cristina Zabala were wed on November 14, 1964, in the San Fernando Catholic Church in Carolina.

Roberto Clemente Night

ROBERTO WAS VERY happy. He and Vera were delighted with the new home that they had bought in Rio Piedras. The house was on top of one of the highest hills for miles around, and the view was spectacular. Roberto could stand on the balcony and see the Atlantic Ocean, the ships in the harbor, and the mountains on the east. The house had a small bridge from the front door to the road over a small dip in the ground.

Roberto had only one concern. He was

afraid that his friends from the barrio, his old neighborhood, might not come to see him in this fine home. He did not need to worry. The house was always open to his friends, and he and Vera had many visitors.

Roberto spent the winter of 1964–65 settling into his new home. He also managed and played with the San Juan Senadores in the Winter League. Even though he had become an important major league player in the United States, he played ball in the winter for his fans in Puerto Rico.

But then it seemed as if all of Roberto's good luck had run out. One day as he was mowing the lawn, a rock was kicked up by the mower and flew against his right thigh. He fell to the ground, clutching his leg. With difficulty, he turned off the mower and managed to stumble into the house, where he stretched out in pain on the floor.

The All-Star Game for the Winter League was played only a few weeks after his accident, and though his leg still hurt he felt he should be in it.

"Perhaps you should not try to play in the All-Star Game, since your leg feels so painful. Maybe it is not really healed," Vera said. She turned out to be correct.

Roberto shook his head. "I feel I should play. All the fans are expecting me to, and I don't want to let them down."

Afterward, Roberto was sorry that he'd decided to play in the All-Star Game. He played hard, which was the only way he knew how, and the fans were cheering him enthusiastically. Suddenly, the mood changed when Roberto's leg gave out as he was running out a base hit. When he went down, there was a collective gasp from the fans as they rose to their feet to see what had happened to their hero.

Roberto was unable to get to his feet. The other players gathered round and helped him off the field. He had a torn ligament and couldn't walk. On January 15, 1965, Roberto had surgery to mend his leg.

Then, on March 1, just when his leg was better and he was supposed to report to the Pirates for spring training, he was in the hospital again. This time he had a temperature of 105 degrees. The doctors didn't know whether he had malaria or typhoid fever or both.

Roberto was so ill in the hospital that his doctors did not feel he should even think about playing baseball for a whole year! But Roberto would not hear of it. When he finally went home to finish his recovery, Roberto also started to get ready to return to practice. He would be a little late, but he would definitely be there. "I need to gain my strength so that I'll be ready to play," he said as he tried to walk and exercise a bit.

"Roberto," Vera said, "why don't you take this year off from baseball so that you can really regain your health?" Vera was worried about him and tried to encourage him to rest and take the year to grow strong again.

Roberto shook his head—he just could not give up baseball for a year. Though he was thin and weakened from his illness, he reported for practice, against the advice of his doctors and the wishes of Vera.

In 1965 the Pirates had a new manager, Harry Walker. This was a pleasant change for Roberto after all the years of disagreeing with Danny Murtaugh. Walker treated Roberto with respect and said that he wished he had a dozen players like him. He added, "He's high-spirited, a thoroughbred. He needs to be treated differently."

Walker gave Roberto whatever he wanted. For example, Roberto wanted clay instead of sand in the batter's box, explaining that his feet slipped on the sand. So Walker had clay put in. To thank him, Clemente went on a batting flurry. During an 11-day period at home in June, he hit .444 with 5 home runs.

Two of the home runs flew over an enormous, iron exit gate in right-center field, 436 feet from home plate. As far as anyone could remember, no one had ever hit two home runs over that gate before.

In 1965 Roberto had the league's highest batting average and won his third batting title. That same season, it became clear that Roberto Clemente was becoming a leader for the young players on the team. If a young player had a problem, Roberto would take him aside, talk to him quietly, and help him solve the problem. Roberto was proving himself to be not only an outstanding player, but also a kind, caring person.

Finally, on November 16, 1966, Roberto received the recognition he deserved for his great playing. It was announced that the sportswriters had voted the Most Valuable Player award to Roberto Clemente! Though he still felt bitter about losing out in 1960, he was pleased to receive the award. "It is the highest honor a player can hope for, but I was expecting it."

During the off-season, Roberto once again returned to his home in Puerto Rico. He loved being back in his own country. There were so many things he enjoyed. He loved seeing old friends. He had many hobbies in addition to playing baseball in the Winter League. He wrote poetry. He liked to play the organ. He worked in ceramics and made driftwood sculptures.

He also was interested in the people of his country, and tried to think of ways he could help them. One thing he especially loved to do was to visit children in the hospital. Roberto also never forgot his teacher, Señora Caceres, and when he was in Puerto Rico he always went to visit her. One time when he went to her house, he found her so ill she could not get out of bed. He picked her up in his arms and drove her to the doctor. He took her to the doctor many times until she was

able to walk again. And he paid all of her doctor bills. Señora Caceres wanted to pay, but Roberto would not let her.

When he and his family traveled, Roberto would always try to meet the local people and understand how they lived. One time when he was on a trip to Nicaragua, Roberto said, "I like it here because it's like Puerto Rico was many years ago." He felt a strong connection to Nicaragua, which he never forgot.

In 1967 he won his fourth batting title with his highest average ever, .357. In one amazing game, he hit three homers and drove in all of the seven Pittsburgh Pirates runs in an 8–7 loss to Cincinnati. It was one of the most terrific games of his career, certainly—"But not my best. I don't count this one. We lost."

With all of the recognition Roberto was receiving, including the respect of his fellow players and his team manager, and the loyalty of the Pittsburgh fans, Roberto was feeling very good. However, there were still experiences of discrimination which angered and hurt him deeply.

One time when he and Vera were in New York, they stopped in a store to look at some furniture for their home in Pittsburgh. The cheapest items were on the first floor, and each floor up had progressively more expensive things. Roberto and Vera started to go up to the eighth floor, which had the furniture they wanted. A salesman stopped them and said, "You can't afford the things up there. You should look at the cheaper furniture on the first floor."

Roberto happened to have five thousand dollars in his pocket because they were on their way to England. He took it out of his pocket and showed it to the salesman, who was shocked at the large amount of money. Another person who was standing nearby said to the salesman, "Don't you know this is

Roberto Clemente, the baseball star?"

The embarrassed salesman apologized. "I am so sorry! Please let me show you the furniture you want to see. I thought you were just another Puerto Rican."

Roberto turned on his heels, and with his arm around Vera, walked out of the store!

In 1970 Danny Murtaugh returned to the Pirates as manager. But this time around Murtaugh had only admiration for Roberto Clemente's ballplaying.

Roberto was invaluable to the team, from his leadership role to his consistent batting and outstanding fielding. From 1969 through 1971, Clemente hit .345, .352, and .341, respectively.

On July 24, 1970, in the new Three Rivers Stadium, which had replaced old Forbes Field, the Pittsburgh Pirates honored Clemente with a Roberto Clemente Night. The stands were packed with more than forty-three thousand fans who had come for the game and festivities. Many awards and gifts were presented to Roberto. Thousands of dollars had been collected, and he asked that the money be given to the Pittsburgh Children's Hospital.

Roberto's ninety-year-old father, Melchor Clemente, and his mother, Luisa, were there. His beautiful wife, Vera, and his three handsome young sons were also there. Hundreds of Puerto Ricans came from the island, bringing with them a scroll signed by over three hundred thousand people!

The Pirates' Latin players honored him by coming up one at a time to touch his shoulder and pay their respects.

He went on to have two base hits in the game and to make two dramatic sliding catches. In the ninth inning, with the Pirates leading by nine runs and with two outs, the manager took him out of the lineup. As he slowly ran in from right field, all of the fans in the stadium were on their feet, cheering and applauding and shouting, "Arriba! Arriba!"

Roberto Clemente felt embraced by the affection which the fans were pouring out to him. He later said, "In a moment like this you can see a lot of years in a few minutes. I don't know if I cried, but I'm not ashamed to cry. We are a sentimental people. I don't have words to say how I feel when I step on that field and know that so many are behind me, and know that I represent my island and Latin America."

World Champions

THE 1971 SEASON started out well and got better and better. This was the year during which the whole country saw that Roberto Clemente was one of the very best baseball players of all time.

In the tense race for the pennant, Roberto helped keep up the team's spirits with his leadership. He encouraged the other players when they were feeling down. During the few minutes in the locker room before they went out on the field, everyone would focus on him.

Clemente also inspired his team members with his outstanding play. One time in Houston he made a fantastic catch in the eighth inning to keep the tying run from scoring. Clemente ran for the corner, leaped high into the air, and caught the ball just as he slammed into the brick wall. The fans jumped to their feet and cheered! One old-time sportswriter said, "It was the greatest catch I ever saw. What guts . . . and to have held the ball."

That catch, and his two-run homer, won the game.

The Pirates won the pennant for the first time since 1960 and were going to the World Series. Everyone was predicting that the Baltimore Orioles would win the Series easily. In 1970 the Orioles had taken the World Series from the Reds in five games. And their 1971 team looked even better.

The Orioles won the first two games, which were played in Memorial Stadium in

Baltimore, and there were those who predicted that the Pirates would not win a single game.

But that changed with Game 3, which was played in Pittsburgh's new Three Rivers Stadium. The skillful pitching of Steve Blass held the Orioles to only one run, and the Pirates defeated the Orioles 5–1.

The fourth game was the first World Series game ever played at night under the lights, and was watched by over sixty million people on national television. Fans all over the country were amazed by Roberto's three hits in four at bats. The Pirates won by a score of 4–3. The Series was tied; each team had won two games.

The next game, Nelson Briles of the Pirates pitched a terrific game. The Orioles didn't get any runs, and the Pirates won 4-0. Roberto Clemente got the last hit to drive in the fourth run. It was the twelfth straight Series game in which Clemente had hit safely!

Games 6 and 7 went back to Baltimore. By now the Orioles knew they would not win this Series as easily as they had thought. Though Roberto's plays in the sixth game were spectacular, Baltimore won in ten innings. Now they were tied at three games apiece, and the next and last game would decide which team would be the champion.

In the seventh game, Clemente produced the first run in the fourth inning with a homer that flew high over the left-center-field fence. In the eighth inning the Pirates got their second run. Steve Blass pitched an outstanding game, giving up only one run in the bottom of the eighth.

In a brilliantly played seventh game, the Pirates won the World Series. Their fans were ecstatic!

The World Series gave the nation's base-ball fans the chance to find out just how mar-velous Roberto was on the field. All over the country fans learned what Pittsburgh Pirates enthusiasts had always known. No sportswriter could deny his ability; no manager could overlook that he gave his all to the game.

Clemente was in a class by himself. He hit safely in all seven World Series games, batted .414, slugged two home runs, knocked in four runs, made two incredible catches, ran full speed, and played his heart out!

Roberto was named the Most Valuable Player in the Series. *Sport* magazine named him the Outstanding Player in the World Series, and he also won the Babe Ruth Award, which is given to the MVP of the Series.

After the game, he said to reporters, "I want everyone in the world to know this is the way I play all of the time. All season, every season, I give everything I have to this game." Any television viewer who'd just seen Clemente knew it was true!

In the television interviews, Roberto said,

"Before I say anything, I want to say something in Spanish to my mother and father." To his parents, Luisa and Melchor Clemente in Puerto Rico, he said, *"En este, el momento mas grande de mi vida, les pido la bendición"*—"On this, the proudest day of my life, I ask your blessing."

On September 30, 1972, Roberto joined that small, select group of players to have three thousand hits in their baseball career when he batted a curveball solidly into left center. The fans leaped to their feet screaming with joy over the accomplishment. The cheering went on and on. Roberto ran to second base and stood there. He tipped his black Pirates' cap to the crowd as he faced them. He dedicated the hit to the fans of Pittsburgh and Puerto Rico and to Roberto Marin, the man who had encouraged him all along the way. Umpire Doug Harvey gave the ball to Clemente, who gave it to first-base coach Don Leppert.

In all its glory, the scoreboard blazed 3000! No one could know that this hit would be his last.

That fall Clemente returned home to manage an amateur Puerto Rican baseball team. He always enjoyed working with young people. He had a dream of building a "Sports City" for the children and young people of Puerto Rico. He thought there should be at least one sport there that each child could enjoy. Then he would have the best coaches for each of the sports. He spent a lot of time thinking about how he would plan Sports City.

In November Roberto and Vera went with the Puerto Rican team to the world amateur baseball championships in Nicaragua. Vera said that the people were extremely nice to them on that trip.

Roberto had a special feeling for Nicaragua. When he saw barefoot boys in the streets, living in one-room houses with large families, it brought back memories of his own childhood. It reminded him of the way it had been when he was a boy and his father worked in the sugarcane fields in Carolina.

Soon after Roberto returned to Puerto Rico, a disastrous earthquake struck Nicaragua, on December 23, 1972. Much of the capital city, Managua, was destroyed. More than five thousand people were killed and twenty thousand were injured. Many thousands more were left homeless.

That very day Roberto Clemente volunteered to be the chairman in Puerto Rico of the effort to gather food, clothing, and medical supplies for the victims in Nicaragua. He worked long hours collecting money, food, clothing and supplies. He personally asked friends and strangers for help. He went door-to-door in his neighborhood to ask for donations.

He worked without rest, packing and loading the boxes to be shipped. He made arrangements with the airlines to fly the donations to Nicaragua. While everyone was celebrating the Christmas holidays, Roberto Clemente was working long, hard days trying to get the supplies to the poor victims of the earthquake.

Word came back that many of the donations being sent to Nicaragua were not getting to the victims. Roberto thought about the many friends he and Vera had made while they were there. He thought especially about one young orphan boy whom he had met when he had visited a hospital. Clemente and other members of the team had donated money to buy the artificial legs the boy needed.

Roberto wondered whether that boy and the other children in the hospital had survived the earthquake. He wondered whether they had received the food and medicine. And he thought about all the other children and babies who were hurt and without homes.

Roberto decided that he himself would go on the plane to deliver the supplies, so that he could make sure that the poor people who needed help were receiving the food, clothing, and medical supplies. No one would dare to steal relief supplies in the presence of someone as well known as Roberto Clemente.

* * *

On December 31, 1972, Roberto Clemente and four other men boarded an old DC-7 cargo plane, crammed with all the humanitarian supplies for the victims of the earthquake. Minutes after 9:00 P.M. the plane took off. Soon after the plane had engine problems and lost speed rapidly. The pilot radioed the tower that he was returning to San Juan, but the plane never reached the airport. It fell into the sea, and all those on board lost their lives.

New Year's Day, 1973, in Puerto Rico was to have been a day of celebration, with the inauguration of a new governor. Instead, the inauguration was canceled, and the day became a day of mourning for Roberto Clemente.

A Terrible Loss

THE WORLD WAS stunned by the tragedy of Roberto Clemente's death on a mission of mercy. Many people payed honor to him. One of the greatest honors was to be voted into the National Baseball Hall of Fame just three months after his death. Normally a player could not be voted in for at least five years after the end of his active career. For Roberto, this rule was waived. On March 20, 1973, the baseball writers voted to include Roberto Clemente in the Baseball Hall of Fame.

Roberto Clemente was enshrined in the Hall of Fame on August 6, 1973, at Cooperstown, New York. Vera and their three young sons—Roberto Jr., Luis, and Enrique—watched with great pride and sadness. Baseball Commissioner Bowie Kuhn said in his tribute that Roberto Clemente was indeed the perfect and classic ballplayer, but also a man who had great pride and deep caring for his fellow man. Kuhn continued his high praise, and then said that there were simply not adequate words to describe him.

It seemed an unusual coincidence, but Roberto's childhood idol, Monte Irvin, was inducted into the Baseball Hall of Fame on the same day.

Roberto achieved so many distinctions in the sport of baseball. He was the first Latin American to be voted into the Baseball Hall of Fame. In the hundred-plus years history of major league baseball, he was only the eleventh man to achieve three thousand hits.

In 1966 he was voted the Most Valuable Player of the National League. He was the batting champion of the National League in 1961, 1964, 1965 and 1967. For twelve seasons, from 1961 through 1972, he was the winner of the Gold Glove for fielding excellence.

Roberto Clemente batted above .300 for thirteen seasons. For his entire big league career, from 1955 through 1972, his average was .317. He played in twelve major league All-Star Games from 1960 through 1972.

He hit safely in all fourteen games of the 1960 and 1971 World Series. He won the Babe Ruth Award for his excellent play in the 1971 World Series.

He tied the National League record by hitting three triples in one game, a record he still shares today. He led the National League in assists five times.

Roberto Clemente was and still is the all-time leader of the Pittsburgh Pirates in games played, at-bats, hits, singles, and total bases. On April 5, 1973, the Pittsburgh Pirates, in a ceremony at Three Rivers Stadium, retired Clemente's number 21 and gave his jersey to Vera and Luisa Clemente.

In July of 1994 the Pittsburgh Pirates held dedication ceremonies for a twelve-foot bronze statue of Roberto Clemente at Three Rivers Stadium.

Roberto Clemente was not only one of the finest ballplayers ever, both because of his abilities and his dedication to always playing at his very best; he was also a man who cared deeply about his family, his countrymen, and people everywhere.

His life centered on his family: his three young sons and his wonderful wife, Vera. He always had the deepest respect and love for his parents as well. "When I was a boy, I realized what lovely persons my father and mother were," Roberto said. "I learned the right way to live. I never heard hate for anybody in my house. I never heard my mother say a bad word to my father, or my father to my mother."

The people of his country were very important to him. During his off-season he traveled around the island running baseball clinics as a way of reaching out to kids. How exciting it was for young boys to learn to play baseball with a famous baseball star like Roberto Clemente! He went to the neighborhoods of many villages and towns to talk about the importance of sports. He also talked about the importance of being a good citizen and of respecting one's mother and father. Oftentimes he would talk with the boys and their fathers together.

Roberto Clemente's dream was to have a Sports City—*Ciudad Deportiva*—where youngsters could go to play all kinds of sports. Under the direction of Vera and his son Roberto, his dream has been fulfilled.

His legacy lives on in the ongoing work of

Ciudad Deportiva. Sports City continues to grow and to be a center for youngsters and an opportunity for them to participate in the sports they love. The 304-acre campus has a track-and-field stadium, tennis and basketball courts, a swimming pool, and an indoor facility for music, art, and dance. The baseball diamonds at the center of Sports City are a four-field complex with a tower in the middle.

Sports City serves over one hundred thousand children and adults each year. Vera Clemente said that she felt the responsibility to give children the opportunity to become not just stars, but good citizens.

Kids come by the busloads to learn and to have fun. And many go on to play professional sports. Some of the most outstanding players in professional baseball today have come through the programs at Ciudad Deportiva or have played in tournaments there. This group includes Juan Gonzales,

Ivan Rodriguez, Edgar Martinez, Carlos Baerga, Sandy Alomar, Benito Santiago, Roberto Alomar, Ruben Sierra, and José Canseco. Many other atheletes have received athletic scholarships to universities in the States.

Roberto Clemente thought that it was important to make things better on this earth if you had the opportunity. Vera Clemente took advantage of the opportunity Roberto had opened up and brought his dream to reality. And true to that dream, Sports City has made life better for thousands of young people.

Roberto's Stats

Roberto Walker Clemente • #21 • Pittsburgh Pirates • Outfielder (1955–1972) • Height: 5-11 • Weight: 175 • Batted: Right • Threw: Right • Born: August 18, 1934 in Carolina, PR • Died: December 31, 1972 • 11th player in major league history to record 3,000 hits • First Hispanic player elected to the Hall of Fame (1973) • National League Most Valuable Player in 1966 • 12-time National League All-Star • Winner of 12 Gold Glove Awards • Winner of four National League batting titles • Hit better than .300 in 13 different seasons • Collected more than 200 hits in four different seasons • Hit safely in all 14 World Series games in which he appeared • Named World Series MVP in 1971 after batting .414 • Led all National League outfielders in assists five times • Pirates' all time leader in the following categories: Games (2,433), At-Bats (9,454), Hits (3,000), Singles (2,154), Total Bases (4,492) • Drafted from Dodgers' Montreal farm club in November 1954 • Killed in a plane crash attempting to fly relief supplies to earthquake victims in Nicaragua • Uniform number retired by the Pirates in 1973

Lifetime Records

Yr. Club	G	AB	R	H	2B	3B	HR	RBI	AVG.
55 Pittsburgh (NL)	124	474	48	121	23	11	5	47	.255
56 Pittsburgh (NL)	147	543	66	169	30	7	7	60	.311
57 Pittsburgh (NL)	111	451	42	114	17	7	4	30	.253
58 Pittsburgh (NL)	140	519	69	150	24	10	6	50	.289
59 Pittsburgh (NL)	105	432	60	128	17	7	4	50	.296
60 Pittsburgh (NL)	144	570	89	179	22	6	16	94	.314
61 Pittsburgh (NL)	146	572	100	201	30	10	23	89	.351•

Lifetime Records cont.

Yr. Club	G	AB	R	H	2B	3B	HR	RBI	AVG.
62 Pittsburgh (NL)	144	538	95	168	28	9	10	74	.312
63 Pittsburgh (NL)	152	600	77	192	23	8	17	76	.320
64 Pittsburgh (NL)	155	622	95	211★	40	7	12	87	.339•
65 Pittsburgh (NL)	152	589	91	194	21	14	10	65	.329•
66 Pittsburgh (NL)	154	638	105	202	31	11	29	119	.317

67 Pittsburgh (NL)	147	585	103	209•	26	10	23	110	.357•
68 Pittsburgh (NL)	132	502	74	146	18	12	18	57	.291
69 Pittsburgh (NL)	138	507	87	175	20	12•	19	91	.345
70 Pittsburgh (NL)	108	412	65	145	22	10	14	60	.352
71 Pittsburgh (NL)	132	522	82	178	29	8	13	86	.341
72 Pittsburgh (NL)	102	378	68	118	19	7	10	60	.312
Major League Totals	2433	9454	1416	3000	440	166	240	1305	.317

• = Led League
★ = Tied the league
    lead with Curt Flood

Championship Series

Yr. Club	G	AB	R	H	2B	3B	HR	RBI	AVG.
70 Pittsburgh (NL)	3	14	1	3	0	0	0	1	.214
71 Pittsburgh (NL)	4	18	2	6	0	0	0	4	.333
72 Pittsburgh (NL)	5	17	1	4	1	0	1	2	.235

World Series

Yr. Club	G	AB	R	H	2B	3B	HR	RBI	AVG.
60 Series	7	29	1	9	0	0	0	3	.310
71 Series	7	29	3	12	2	1	2	4	.414

—Courtesy of the Pittsburgh Pirates

Glossary

All-Star Game–the annual interleague game played each July between players selected as the best at their position in their league.

American League–one of the two major leagues of baseball teams. The American League was founded in 1901.

at bat–the number of times a batter comes up to the plate. For player statistics, an at bat is not counted if the batter walks, sacrifices, is hit by a pitched ball, or is interfered with by the catcher.

batting average–the total number of hits a player gets divided by his total number of at bats. The standard of excellence is an average of .300 (three hundred) or better.

games–the number of games played.

hits–a ball batted into fair territory that allows the batter to reach base safely without the help of an error. The very best players average 200 hits a season.

SB–Stolen Base–when a runner advances one base safely while the ball is being pitched to the batter

2B–Second Base–double; a hit on which the batter goes to second base.

3B–Third Base–triple; a hit on which the batter goes to third base.

HR–Home Run–a four-base hit on which the batter scores. The batter and his team are awarded a run when he has touched all four bases.

National League–one of the two major leagues of baseball teams. The National League was founded in 1876.

run–A run is scored for the team and the player after he has touched all of the bases and arrives home safely.

RBI–run batted in–a run that scores as a result of a player's batting, whether he gets an out, hits safely, sacrifices, walks, or is hit by a pitch. When a home run is made with the bases loaded, the batter would be credited with four runs batted in.

World Series–the games played between the American and National League pennant winners at the end of the season to decide the World Championship. The first team to win four games is the winner. The World Series has been played since 1903.